I0520183

PLUM
BOTTOM

PLUM BOTTOM

ESTHER ESCOTT

Copyright © 2016 Esther Escott
All rights reserved.

ISBN: 0692680101
ISBN 13: 9780692680100
Library of Congress Control Number: 2016905390
EscottBooks, Walnut Creek, CA

To my husband, Charlie,
for providing just what I needed
in writing this book—another head,
and for making me laugh.

.

With thanks to my editor,
Paul Weisser, Ph.D.,
who not only polished my prose, but also
helped me to become a better writer.

Laney Mahler grew up in a lowland part of town called Plum Bottom. As a child, never seeing that colloquial name in print, she thought it was spelled "plumb" bottom. Not very happy about living in the plumb bottom of the town, she was glad years later to learn that the area was named for wild plum trees that had once grown there, on the wide, flat valley bordered by a creek and a river.

THE LORD HATETH

"Mom Angelo, I think I know this chicken!" Mom and Laney crossed the barnyard, Mom carrying two leghorns dangling head-down, and Laney, six years old, trotting barefooted beside her. The hen nearest Laney cocked an eye up at her as if wondering where the next horror would come from. "Wasn't it the little pullet that used to follow me around? It used to help me find eggs in the rock pile!"

Mom plodded on, her back so bent that her top half was almost parallel to the ground. The set of her little puckered mouth warned Laney that she was in a mood for the hard truth. Truth, the way Laney liked it, was soft as mashed potatoes, to be worked and shaped and often greatly improved. As in this case, when the plain truth—that she pitied the chickens— would never stop Mom from killing them.

Approaching the shed, where the ax hung, Laney thought faster. "We used to sit under the hemlock and keep each other company. You know that little cut-cut-cut sound they make? I got so I could understand this one, almost."

"No! Stop-a-you! You-a *feeb*-a!"

"Huh-*uh*, Mom." She stepped back as Mom approached the shed door. Inside hung the ax, glinting sharp. Mom lifted one hand to the door latch, setting off a frenzy of squawking and flapping. The shaken hen strained upward, trying to right itself, and when it settled again, its beak dripped milky fluid. "Mom Angelo, do chickens throw up?"

"Ya. Ya. Go!" She jerked her straggly, gray top-knot toward Laney's home, across the road. "G'wan! Shoo!"

Laney despaired, watching Mom's stockings, rolled into brown doughnuts around her ankles. She wondered if it would help if she cried. Mom stepped in and closed the door on her as if she had already left.

So Laney turned and ran. Hotfooted it across the dirt, past the milkhouse, past the whitewashed stones, toward the road, running lightly on legs that reminded her how strong she was. Near the gate she ducked aside under the low, sprawling branches of the hemlock tree into a needle-lined nest.

She sat down, hugged her knees, clenched her eyes shut, and looked back deep inside her mind. *Dear God our help in ages past*, she prayed, *please let those chickens go free*. Rocking back and forth, she watched the light patterns inside her brain and thought of the chickens' necks, thin as bean poles inside their oily, fright-raised feathers. She waited for the hacking blow of the ax.

Instead came a humming sound. It grew to a rumble; a car was coming over the bridge. Few cars travelled the valley road, and it didn't sound like her Dad's old Chev or either of the Angelos' trucks. Still no ax blow. The car came nearer with that strange engine noise till she couldn't stand it and crept through the branches out to the road. As she stood squinting in the sun, she saw with a jolt that it was the police car. It stopped at the Angelos', between Laney and home, causing her to scramble back under the hemlock.

But when the policeman stepped out, she recognized him and her fear lessened. Buck Schrock, young and still new at his job after a couple years. People said he wasn't very forceful, but he was nice. Curiosity drew her out again.

"Hello there," he called.

She stood up slowly, embarrassed because of her bare legs and old, faded sunsuit.

"Bet you're Harv Mahler's girl, ain't you, the younger one?"

She nodded, watching her mother come across their front yard. She was almost running, and Laney knew why—the police car meant trouble, and Mom Angelo, who spoke little English, was home alone.

"Anybody home here at Angelos'?" Buck asked Laney.

In the barnyard, the shed door opened and a squawking chicken flew out, followed by Mom Angelo. Seeing the police car, she stood straighter as the other chicken ran out the door. "My man-a, my man-a!" she cried.

"I'm coming, Mom!" cried Laney's mother, changing course to run around the milkhouse.

Laney suddenly recalled a tale that Pop Angelo had once gotten sick, working up on the hill, and they'd brought him down in the police car. "Is Pop Angelo hurt?" she asked Buck.

"No, no, nothing like that," he said, looking flustered.

"It's not Pop Angelo, Mom! It's about something else," her mother said, leading the old woman over, trembling and moaning.

"Listen, I didn't mean to upset her, I'm just looking for Billy Schradel. He used to work for the Angelos, I believe."

"Yes, we all know him." Mrs. Mahler looked angry with Buck for scaring Mom. "You won't find him around here, though. He's at the County Farm."

"Not anymore, he ain't. He run off."

"Not again!" The shock on her mother's face surprised Laney. She thought back a year or so to Billy, clumping down the road, a skinny, toothless old man who never grew up. Sometimes she had come over to the fence with her parents and her older sister, Carol, to talk. She had even let Billy tweak her braids. But she had learned to stay clear of his long arms. Once they had lifted her over the fence to have her cheeks rubbed on his whiskery chin.

"Well, we haven't seen him," Mrs. Mahler said. "Mom, he's looking for poor old Billy Schradel. He's run off from the County Farm again."

"Ahh," she nodded.

"I guess I ought to talk to Mr. Angelo," Buck said, gazing past the gray-and-white farm buildings gleaming in the sun.

"They're up on the hill in the truck patch. Pop, Leo, and the girls. The girls drive tractor and work like men." As Buck turned aside to blow his nose, Mrs. Mahler stood thinking. Then she said, "You know, that last time Billy was here, he told us he had a sister in Maryland who would keep him."

Laney looked up. She'd thought the sister had died.

"'Scuse me," Buck mumbled, sniffing hard. "Well, I wish to heck he'd gone down there, then. Would'a saved me a peck o' trouble."

"He's just a harmless old man."

Laney, intently watching his face, saw him grow uneasy. "It's for his own good, Ma'am. You know how he is. At the Farm he gets fed regular."

"He hated the Farm! He said he'd rather die than be sent back there." Mrs. Mahler's voice broke, filling Laney with alarm. "He cried to Harv and me, that last time he got out, cried in front of us!"

"Mama, let's go home," Laney said, pulling on her hand.

"I'm sure sorry, Mrs. Mahler. That's all I can say. I have the folks in town to contend with, you know, not to mention the county."

Mrs. Mahler nodded—silent, Laney knew, because her tears still threatened, and also because there was little one could say at the mention of the county.

Buck asked if she would just tell Mr. Angelo that Billy was loose, and call the office if he showed up. She replied that she guessed she could do that much. He apologized again, and sneezed as he left. They watched him back the police car in the Mahlers' driveway and pull out toward the bridge in a cloud of dust.

"C'mon, Mom," Mrs. Mahler said sadly. "I'll help you catch those chickens."

But Mom waved her aside, embarrassed now, smoothing her apron and pushing back stray hairs. "I-ee, scared-a me, my man he-ee...." She appealed upward to her taller neighbor for understanding.

"I know, Mom, you were afraid Pop had another heart attack."

"Ya. Ya."

"It's alright. I was scared, too."

Laney and her mother went home then, Laney somber to see that there wasn't much left of the day, and what there was, was ruined. There could be no joy for her on a day when her mother cried. At least, the chickens were free. She wondered if God Our Father was helping old Billy, too. After all, like the hymn said, His eyes were on the sparrow.

After supper, with the Mahlers' house still rich with the smells of coffee and fried ham, Laney sped up playing "Two Puppies" on the piano.

"That's too fast!" called Carol, ten, from the dining room table, where she was busy with her homework.

Sighing impatiently, Laney started the song again, more slowly, but pounding harder. She was anxious to get outside before dark. "Mama, am I done yet?" she called to the kitchen.

"That's a half-hour, Elaine. You can go play a little before bedtime."

As Laney ran onto the front porch, she heard the rattling of cans in the milkhouse. The girls would be there after working on the hill all day, and possibly handsome, curly-haired Leo. She jumped from the porch into the grass and ran around to the backyard for apples. A quick search under the trees showed no fallen fruit; few had fallen yet. Tarzan she was, climbing the tree—foot up, hand over hand, leg up, knee over, and slide around the trunk. She knew every step and handhold by heart. Muscular and brave, she sat astride the limb, puffing with her mighty chest. Lion Girl she was—no, Leopard Girl. Her chin lifted, brows raised. She was beautiful, too.

Light was fading! She picked the green apples, dropping them inside the bib of her sunsuit. Rich, joyful laughter came from the milkhouse. Hurry! She started the difficult descent with her chestful of apples bumping her knee. A couple dropped down and out the leg hole. No matter. On the ground, she held her lumpy front as she streaked across the grass to the road.

"Maria! Josie! Marcella!"

They were heading for the house. She saw their jeans and work shirts in the yellow light from the milkhouse. Maria, who was soon to be married, had tied her shirt bottoms under her round breasts. The oldest, Marcella, was tall and bossy like her father. The youngest and prettiest, Josie, had just graduated from high school. Leo, a working man at nineteen, was nowhere in sight.

"Laney! Come here, sweetheart, give us a look at you!" Maria's voice was husky and warm as honey as she reached for the girl. "Give me a kiss, baby. Umm-a!" Then she squeezed her shoulders. "What do you have in here?"

"I brought you some apples."

"Josie! Come look what Laney brought over! Green apples!"

"They're getting big," said Josie, taking one from Maria. "Next they'll be too ripe."

Laney grinned happily as they crunched the apples with their strong, white teeth. It was a puzzle to her how they could eat the not-quite-ripe apples. Not only were they hard and sour, but she'd heard that green apples could give one the runs. It didn't seem to bother the Angelo girls.

"Supper's ready," Marcella cautioned, but reached for an apple anyway. "Tell us about your adventures, Laney. What did you do today? You were here when Buck Schrock came, weren't you?"

"Yes!" Laney's anger rekindled. "He better not show up around here again!"

"Why, honey? He's just doing his job. You know what he did before he was a cop? He drove a milk truck."

"Look who's standing up for Buck," Josie taunted. "She's sweet on him, yaa, yaa, yaa."

Marcella took a loud, crunching bite of apple.

Maria threw away her core and took Laney's braids in her hands. "Tell us something else, honey. Tell us one of your stories." She looked to the porch, where the light had gone on. "Hurry up, now."

"Well…," Laney thought fast. "I was standing on the bridge today…."

"Yeah?"

"…looking down the river, and there was a basket floating on the water. And there was a little baby in it."

"No!"

"It was one of those reedy clothes baskets. The little baby was wrapped up in a blanket, with its arms sticking out. And it was crying."

"Oh, that's a sad story."

"It looked up at me on the bridge, with its little arms reaching for me. Then the basket bobbed around so, some water ran in."

"Stop, you'll make me cry."

"Then it went out of sight. I couldn't see it anymore, that poor little thing." Laney's throat ached with sorrow.

"That's too sad," said Maria. "Tell us a happy one now, about the tree."

"Tree?" she asked, blinking.

"The elevator tree, where the limb goes up and down and you give people rides."

"Maria! Josafina! Marcella!" Mom called hoarsely from the porch.

"Oh, Mom, leave us alone a minute!" Marcella growled.

"Comin', Mom," Josie called.

"We gotta go," said Maria, patting Laney's cheek with a work-roughened hand.

"Ee-laa-aine, come ho-ome," came a long call from across the road.

The girls called their farewells:

"Play 'Two Puppies' one more time, will you? I love to hear that one."

"Me too, it's my favorite. I can just see those puppies bouncing around."

"Good night, angel girl."

Laney ran home smiling as she pounded up the front porch steps to the welcome light of the living room. Glancing into the dining room, she saw that Carol was gone; probably she was upstairs. Laney slid onto the piano bench and played the song happy and bouncy, just the way the Angelo girls liked it.

Later, in bed, she tried to stay awake, knowing that there might be singing and accordion music from across the road. She pictured Leo holding the accordion, with black curls tumbling over his forehead. Although he never noticed her at all, she liked to be where he was. It made her show off and act silly, which her mother said wasn't ladylike. Carol, who seemed to have no interest in Leo, said it made her look like a real goof. Leo, smiling with dimples in his tan cheeks, faded into the dark.

———

Sunday afternoon, Laney was looking for something to do in the backyard. She picked up a green apple and tried a bite, but had to make a face and spit it out—still too sour. Her sister had gone to a girlfriend's house, her mother was lying down, and her father was snoring gently on the porch swing. Laney hummed to herself as she picked up two other apples that had fallen, and looked around for a third. But there were no more. Gazing up into the tree, she decided it was too hot to climb. So, with an apple in each hand, she started across the road.

The Angelos' house and yard were quiet. The whole world seemed asleep in the Sunday afternoon sunshine. As Laney thought back to the escape of Mom's two leghorns, it occurred to her that she ought to search for them, to see if they were still alive. Mom Angelo might have caught them again and butchered them.

The barnyard was empty except for a few hens in the dirt behind the corncrib, throwing up gray puffs as they dug in. Passing the barn door behind which the bull was tied, she saw that it was ajar. The cows, she knew, were out to pasture until milking time. But the bull should be there. Cautiously she opened the door and peered in. The room was dark, after the bright barnyard, with only a small window for light.

She stepped in. On the far wall, above a pile of hay, hung some blankets and a lantern. She wondered what the blankets were for. Did Pop Angelo cover the bull when it got really cold in the winter? The bull was a furry hump, almost as wide as high. He slowly turned his thick neck to roll an eye toward her, bawled a low note, and turned back again.

A memory tugged at her, a curiosity she'd had for some time. Her knowledge of the male body was limited to those times she had been called into the bathroom when her father was in the tub, to scrub his back. Once she had glimpsed something floating in front of him in the water. Always she had sponged his back in acute embarrassment, and when finished, had tiptoed out and flittered through the hall and down the steps.

Still holding her apples, she stepped closer to the bull. There it hung, a long, pendulous bag. She had glimpsed it before, but never had a chance to really *look*. Further upfront, where the milk bag would have been, was a tuft of hairs. So that was it, then.

A fly bothered the bull's flank, causing him to stir. The bag swung gently. Laney thought a bit, then her hands started rolling her smooth little apples. She tossed one, which touched his leg. Kneeling, she took better aim. This time the apple hit the bag itself, causing the gentle animal to lift a leg in surprise.

"Laney! What the hell! Are you teasing the bull? Throwing apples!" Leo towered over her, blocking the light.

She stood up, thunderstruck.

"I know what you're doing, you little brat! Shame on you!" His face was terrible in anger.

She stood in an agony of embarrassment. "I…. I thought maybe he would like them."

"That's a rotten lie! You weren't throwing them toward his mouth." He grabbed her shoulder in a crushing grip. The pain was unbearable.

"Ow," she said in a small voice.

"Git for home, you little liar!" He shoved her and she fell off-balance, catching onto the door frame. As she darted across the barnyard, she tripped on a rock and nearly fell, then scuttled across the road.

That night she lay in bed so shrunken that she sank into the mattress, making the blanket nearly flat. If she could only disappear, fade down into the bed. They had made her go to evening church, so pale and quiet they'd thought she was coming down with something.

"She has no fever, Harv," her mother had said. "I think she's just tired."

"Has she been eating those green apples?"

"No, she just gives them to the Angelo girls."

"Humph. That's a mistake, too."

"Harv," her mother had cautioned.

So Laney had sat with her family for an hour on a hard wooden pew in the house of God, while the blue sky outside the windows turned dark. Then the choir, in their black robes and gauzy prayer coverings, had sung about a person so deep in sin, he was drowning in it.

The dreadful barn scene kept returning to her mind, so she planned a better ending:

"Please, Leo, it's just me, Laney. I wasn't hurting the bull. I didn't throw those apples hard, just easy."

"Oh, it's you, Laney. I didn't recognize you." He smiles, reaching for her hand. *"Would you let me walk you to your house?"*

But no, that was impossible. Thinking further, it pained her to recall how mean Leo had been. Her shoulder had a sore spot now, probably a bruise.

At the thought, she grew cross. *"It's me, Laney. Who do you think you're yelling at? Your stupid bull kicked me! It's a wonder I didn't stick a pitchfork in him! Now get out of my way, I'm going to the house to tell Mom Angelo on you!"*

But it was no use. Her protective rage slipped away, baring the guilty shame. "Liar," he had called her, and of course, she was. How could she have told the truth when the truth was so terrible? And why did it have to be Leo? It could have been Mom Angelo, or even Pop. But Leo?! The thought made her squirm under the covers, with hot tears springing anew.

"Elaine, are you asleep?" her mother said at the door.

Laney first pretended to be asleep, but then, yearning for comfort, she said huskily, "No, I'm awake."

Her mother entered the room and sat on the bed. "What are you lying so flat for?"

Laney disturbed the flat blanket to reach out for her mother's hand.

"Elaine, I've been thinking. Did something happen over at the Angelos today that frightened you?"

Laney's heart began thumping. "No. Not that I can remember."

"Are you sure? You ran home so fast, and then you seemed so quiet all evening. Tell me, Elaine. You can tell your mother."

"It was just something in the barnyard." The back of her mind despaired, but her mouth kept talking. "The tractor. I was playing behind it, and it moved, just a little. I got up and ran, but it kept moving. But then it stopped." She lay still and waited.

Her mother sat thinking. "But the ground is all level there."

"Well. . . . Besides, I saw one of the chickens that got away from Mom the other day," she said. "It still looked a little rumpled."

"There wasn't a word of truth in that story, was there?"

"Uh-*huh*!"

Her mother sighed, then tucked Laney's hand back under the blanket. "Elaine, you must never play around the tractor again, hear? Even if it isn't moving. And I want you to remember something, as you grow to be a big girl. The Lord hateth a lying tongue."

Laney nodded. Her mother rose and left, her drooping shoulders showing her worry and, worse, her disappointment.

Laney's tears seeped out again, and her face began working. *How did that hymn go? "I was sinking deep in sin, far from the peaceful shore...."* But later came a little relief: *"Love lifted me, love lifted me...."*

She said the comforting words a few times, and began to feel sleep coming, like soft hands beneath her, buoying her up.

Her mother's voice came quietly through the wall, waking her. "Harv, did you know before yesterday about Billy running off from the Farm?"

"No, that was the first I'd heard it."

"I would never have known, if Buck Schrock hadn't been here. Then I heard tonight that Billy was seen down by the Kingman, picking up garbage. He spends a fair amount of time by the river."

"Who told you that, Vera?"

"One of the Angelo girls."

"Humph. Maybe they made that up. I'm telling you, those girls aren't fit company for Laney."

"Shhh. She gets lonesome with Carol in school, Harv, you know that. When she starts first grade this fall, she'll find children her own age. I like the Angelo girls. They work so hard, and I think she's a little entertainment for them."

"I don't care. They encourage her to tell lies."

"Stories. All children tell stories."

"But where does it stop? She's liable to start believing her stories. Or just lying whenever it suits her. I'm telling you, it's getting to be a problem."

The bed springs rasped as he turned over.

Laney lay straight and rigid in bed. "*Dear God, Our Redeemer*," she whispered, staring into the deep dark of the ceiling. "*I promise I'll never tell another lie.*"

She stayed stiff so long that after a while her body felt cold and hard. Then she carefully rolled over and eased her stomach by curling up into a ball.

———

Monday morning, Laney's head hurt as she stepped outside. The sunlight was so blazing bright, it made her squint. She had wrapped her burden of guilt into a neat package in her mind. It formed a tender lump, which she didn't dare touch for fear of pain. She carried it gingerly, protecting it with plenty of space.

She had put on a good pinafore dress with white shoes and socks, vaguely hoping to feel that she was making a fresh start. Her mother was out back, whitewashing tree trunks, a job that made her sweaty and irritable. She had already been cross with Laney for putting on Sunday clothes.

So Laney wandered out front. On the porch, she knelt quickly behind the bannisters while the tractor and hay wagon roared out from the barnyard and passed her house. Leo, looking strangely relaxed and calm, was at the wheel, Pop was beside him, and the girls were in the wagon. When they were out of sight, Laney stepped down to the sidewalk.

She was watching her skinny legs slant down into her socks, pledging to keep clean all day, when the police car came slowly down the road. It slipped by so stealthily that it raised hardly any dust, and caused her no alarm but only mild surprise. It crept on through the open gate into the Angelos' barnyard.

She wondered if she should call her mother, but remembered how cross she had been. Besides, Mom Angelo wouldn't be frightened this time—Buck Schrock had brought no bad news about Pop yesterday and likely wouldn't today. And Mom would know that he was just looking for Billy again. Laney slowly crossed the road.

But before she got there, the Angelos' screen door banged shut. Mom appeared, hobbling down the steps, her hands working to dry themselves in her apron. "No! No! You go! My man-a, he gone!"

"It's alright, Mom," Laney called as she ran. "He's only looking for Billy!" She caught up with Mom at the police car.

Buck climbed out and closed the door softly. His eyes swept the buildings, silent in the sun, then darted across the street to check the Mahlers' yard. "Now, don't anybody be frightened. You know I won't hurt anyone. But I got word Billy was seen down here, and I've got to check it out."

"Everyone's gone, Mr. Schrock!" Laney shouted, alarmed by Mom's fright. "You came again when nobody's home but Mom!"

"Well, I'm sorry I missed them," he said, his eyes shifting uneasily. "But Mr. Angelo knows me. I'm sure he wouldn't mind if I look around."

"I'll go get my mother, then."

"No! No, don't bother her. I won't be here that long."

Mom moaned with each breath. Laney took her arm, saying, "It's alright, Mom, you don't have to worry about anything."

But Mom pulled roughly away from her, shaking her head. Laney frowned, watching Mom's frightened mouth pinching and working. Suddenly a terrible knowledge swept over her like cold water.

"I'm just takin' a quick look, ma'am," Buck said, "don't you worry, now." He opened the milkhouse door, looked around inside, and closed it again.

Next they watched helplessly as he searched the open shed, squeezing himself around among the plows and harrows. Then he paused to blow his nose in his handkerchief.

Suddenly, Laney remembered blankets. Her heart began pounding harder. "There are good hiding places in the chicken house," she called. "I hide in there sometimes myself, playing."

Buck nodded, starting toward the chicken house. To Laney's satisfaction, he blundered in, too confidently for a stranger, causing a tumult of flapping and squawking inside.

He emerged quickly in a cloud of dust, sneezing violently. But even as he touched his handkerchief to his swelling eyes, he was studying the barn. Laney's hopes sank as he strode over and disappeared into the cows' long empty room.

Suddenly, Mom turned and ran out the gate. She stood in the empty road, staring after the tractor and wagon, long gone. Then she turned toward Laney. "Go!" She pointed to Laney's house. "Vera! You go!"

Of course! Laney turned and ran toward home.

Suddenly, Mom cried out, "No! No!"

Laney stopped and looked back just as Buck was leaving the cow stalls and approaching the bull's little room. The door was latched. Yesterday it had been ajar.

"Stop!" Laney cried. "Don't go in there!" Her feet carried her swiftly toward him. "You mustn't go in there! The bull's in there!"

"Oh?"

"He's mean! No one ever goes in there but Pop Angelo!"

"Well, he's tied up, isn't he?"

"No! They can't tie him! When they tie him up, he breaks the stall!"

"Lord!" Buck's hand paused at the door latch and drew back. He studied the heavy door, securely latched, and the small, high window. Then he watched Laney sharply while calling over his shoulder to Mom, "Mrs. Angelo, is there a bull in here?"

"Ya! Ya! Da boola!" Her head bobbed.

"Lordy!" He stepped back whistling, and thought for a few seconds. "Well, I guess Billy ain't hardly in *there*, then." He turned around, pausing for a long moment of indecision. Then he scanned the buildings to see if he'd missed any. The yard lay quiet; hens were cautiously stepping back up the ramp to their house.

"Well," he said again, "I guess that's it, then." His red face seemed relieved, and Laney saw in a dim flash that he wished he were still a milk truck driver.

Buck apologized for the intrusion, while Mom gratefully nodded. Then he said goodbye and headed for the car. When he had backed carefully out of the barnyard onto the road, Mom pulled up her apron bottom to wipe her face.

Laney stared down at her white shoes. They and the whitewashed stones glared up at her too brightly. She saw the light turn opposite, like a photo negative; black things looked white, and white things looked black.

An approaching roar grew louder, then the tractor and wagon came hurtling down the road with the men and girls piled on. As it wheeled into the barnyard, the girls jumped off and came running.

"What happened? We saw Buck leave!" Maria called as they reached Mom and Laney.

Mom started jabbering in Italian, gesturing first to the barn and then to Laney. The girls started shouting and laughing in amazement. Suddenly, Mom reached for Laney, pulled her into her bosom, and kissed her with loud smacks on both cheeks.

Leo and Pop had hurried to the bull's room, where Pop opened the door, peered in, and asked a low question.

Josie knelt down in front of Laney, taking her by the shoulders. "Laney, you're a brave girl! You're a hero today!"

"Isn't she clever?" Marcella said, bending over Laney to smooth her hair. "She's got a quick little mind. As quick as a fox."

Still Laney didn't speak.

"Look at her. She's frightened, now that it's all over."

Maria asked her, "What's wrong, honey girl?"

Laney blurted out in an angry and tearful voice, "Nobody was *doing* anything!"

"What do you mean, Laney?" Maria looked confused. "*You* did it! You didn't need any help. You saved Billy, all by yourself."

Laney's mother, who had come running across the road, now met Pop Angelo and Leo at the tractor.

The girls were laughing again with their little black squares for teeth, praising Laney, patting her hair and shoulders.

At last, Laney spoke. "I told another lie."

Vera, who stood with the two men, leaned to one side to peer over at Laney. An anxious frown formed on her face. Then she started hurrying over to her side. Laney started sobbing as her mother bent down to look her closely in the eyes.

"Don't cry, Elaine. Please don't cry." She hugged her gently, then took her hand. "C'mon, honey, let's go home." As they walked away the puzzled Angelo girls called their good-byes.

They crossed the road steadily, hand in hand. By the time they reached the front porch, Laney had stopped sobbing, concentrating on the warmth of her mother's hand.

Her mother seemed to be thinking hard, looking down at her feet as she walked, with her mouth puckering and pinching almost as worriedly as Mom Angelo's.

LANEY JOINS THE DUNKARDS

At twilight, eight-year-old Laney Mahler and her mother, Vera, left the parking lot and hurried to a basement door in the large, brick church. Inside, the organ was playing softly, sadly–hymns like "The Old Rugged Cross", "Love lifted Me", and "Lead Kindly Light"—hymns appropriate for the evening's communion service.

The Church of the Brethren, which was sometimes called the Dunkard Church, stemmed from an old, German sect closely enough aligned with the Amish and Mennonites that these people from outlying farms occasionally attended the church services. The name itself, Dunkard, referred to the church's practice of baptism by immersion. In simpler terms, people were dunked. Laney was slightly bothered by the name, thinking it too close to the word, "drunkard".

This evening, Laney and Vera entered the church basement and stepped into air rich with an aroma that caused Laney to inhale deeply and sigh: roast beef, and lots of it. The large, cement-floored room was filled with white-clothed tables and plain metal chairs, in preparation for the "Love Feast" that was soon to start. Laney was looking forward to it, though she had been forewarned by her sister, Carol, who was twelve, that she'd be served just broth with a little bit of meat and bread in it, and that was it; no use wishing for more.

Vera hustled her up a small, back staircase that passed so near the organ, which was just behind the wall, that the music throbbed in Laney's nervous brain. Tonight, before the Love Feast, she was to be baptized.

They made their way through several connected Sunday School rooms, ending up in one filled with very small chairs. Laney, a third-grader, was surprised; for her dressing area, she'd been placed in what seemed to be a Kindergarten room.

"Go ahead and get undressed," her mother said. "See, here's the robe, on this hook. Lay your clothes on the chairs, and pull the robe on over your head. Okay? Then just wait, and the preacher will come to lead you into the baptistry."

"I have to take off everything, right?" Laney asked.

"Yes. But don't worry, no one can see through these heavy robes. The preacher will have one on, too. To go into the water."

Laney looked at her sharply. Earlier, the preacher had explained the procedure to her and her mother. At home, Carol had explained it further. But suddenly the thought of herself and Reverend Hillman in the water together struck Laney as so peculiar, it was uncomfortable.

It added another facet to her very real fear of being totally submerged. Carol had told her it was nothing to worry about, but Carol had been to a regular pool a few times, where a friend was teaching her how to swim. Laney, having had no place to swim but a deepened hole in a creek that her mother thought was unclean, had never been completely underwater. She had practiced ducking in the bathtub, holding her nose, but had never submerged her face past her ears. And for all she knew, baptism might take longer than the few seconds she had endured dunking her face in the tub.

The baptistry was well known to her; nothing frightening there. It had a back door through which she would enter, and the whole, wide front of it opened into the church auditorium. On the curving back wall, an outdoor scene that she loved had been painted, with beautiful hills and trees. But she knew the baptistry best at Christmas, when the pool area, always empty except for baptisms, was floored over with wood to become a stable for the manger scene.

Vera, a Deaconess in the church, gathered up her purse. "I have to go downstairs now, Laney. I'm sorry I can't stay here with you. But I have to help with the food, you know. Dad's down there now with the grape juice. I'll be coming back up shortly, to sit out front and watch you be baptized. Carol will be there too, with her friend, Doris. Alright, Honey? Are you okay?"

Laney nodded uncertainly.

"You can dress yourself afterward, can't you? Because I'll be hurrying back down. I'll ask Carol to look in on you. Look, there's a towel here to dry yourself with."

"Okay," Laney said, gazing at the floor.

"Good luck, Laney. You'll be fine, I know. Bless you, Sweetheart." Bending down, she held Laney's head in both hands and pressed her warm cheek to Laney's. "I'm so proud of you. You're entering God's church as a real member, you know. Say a little prayer."

With that, her mother left.

Laney looked after her, briefly wishing she could have stayed. But she understood: she had been brought up to understand situations like this. Her mother's job tonight was important, as was her father's. And her mother had seemed nervous, maybe even more so than she, herself. Laney knew that she could take care of herself in many ways. Privately, she believed that she was grownup for her age.

Sitting down on one of the tiny chairs, she unbuckled her patent leather shoes and pulled off her socks. Then, standing, she pulled the dress up over her head, carefully. It was brand new, made of cloth slightly crisp but filmy, in the palest blue. The gathered skirt stood out nicely all around her. It was by far the prettiest dress she'd ever had. She'd been surprised that her mother was willing to pay so much money for it.

Suddenly it struck her that the preacher would be coming for her any minute, and she'd better get that robe on! She whipped off her cotton vest and panties, and laid them on a chair.

The white robe felt heavy as a rug, which was reassuring. It would conceal her well. It was too big, with long sleeves falling past her hands. Holding up the long skirt, she found small stones sewn into the hem. Knowing at once what they were for, she was relieved. For weeks, through her general uneasiness, she had worried that the skirt would float up around her in the water, leaving her completely naked beneath it.

Then it struck her that the preacher, in a robe like this, would be as bare inside it as she! She quickly brushed the thought aside, as unthinkable. Lifting the gown's bottom, she fingered a couple of the stones inside the hem. They were very small. When she stepped into the water and this skirt came floating up, could such little stones hold it down?

Considering it carefully, she feared they would not.

The worry in her mind suddenly grew larger. What an awful situation to be in! Knowing that she was running out of time, she scurried over to the chair that held her underwear, and grabbed her underpants. She struggled with the huge skirt to get her legs into the holes, and then pulled the panties up. Still settling herself, she heard a footstep in the hall. Just in time! He was coming.

"Ah, Laney. How are you? Very good. I see you're ready?" He looked to her for a reply.

"Yes," she said. She was studying his outfit: instead of a cloth gown, he was wearing something like rubber boots that came clear up to his waist.

"Ready to become a member of our church?"

She nodded.

"And do you remember the things we discussed? I'm sure you do. That's a good girl. Let's move right along, then." He started toward the door. "There are two more people being baptized after you, did you know that?" He made it sound interesting.

Laney held up her long skirt and followed him, saying no, she didn't know that.

He lead her through the back door of the baptistry, stepping ahead of her into the water.

There were a few steps; she took them with the preacher holding her hand. The water, as she would later tell her parents, was cold but a little bit warm. Down one step, and another, and she gripped his hand because it wasn't easy to keep her balance.

Finally, she planted her bare feet on the bottom, with the water coming just above her waist. The gown: yes! It did float up around her. Just at first—then it got so heavy with water and stones that it sank.

But she quickly forgot about that. She started taking the long, deep breath.

She was still holding it when he told her to take a deep breath, and it was so late, she had to let that one out and take another one, which wasn't as deep as the first had been.

The preacher spoke her name, loudly enough that the people in the pews could hear. Then he pressed one large hand over her face, covering most of it, and the other hand on the back of her head. One push from behind and down she went, her ears filling completely with water.

Over the bubbling sound, she heard his voice saying, "I baptize thee in the name of the Father—"

And then, up she came. With his hands still over her face and head, he dunked her again in the name of the Son, and finally, a third plunge in the name of the Holy Ghost.

Then she was up for good and he took his hands away. Just in time—she took a good, chest-filling breath of air, and blew it out wetly.

That wasn't hard! Water from her dripping hair poured into her eyes and down her face. Having no towel, she wiped at her face with her hands.

He was beaming at her, in his wonderful, fat-cheeked smile. "Very good, Laney! You did fine! Welcome into the Lord's Kingdom and your own church family." Then, still smiling, he shepherded her up and out of the baptistry. Down the short hallway she strode, carrying her heavy skirt and dripping water on the wooden floor, as he rushed past her to get the towel.

Then she was drying her face and hair, and he was gone. She was alone again in the Kindergarten room. Where was Carol? Maybe she wasn't coming.

When she had gotten out of the gown, she immediately found a problem. It surprised her that she hadn't thought of it earlier. Her underpants were soaking wet. She took them off, and dried herself. Then she started in on the panties, first wringing them out onto the towel.

It helped. They were a little bit dry—no, not really. They were way too wet to put on. What would happen when she sat down? She would have to sit a long while during the Love Feast, and her dress would get wet and crumpled. And it would show! What would people think?

Staring at the worrisome garment, suddenly a completely different thought came into her mind as clearly as if someone had spoken it.

She looked up into the dim space below the ceiling. The baptism was over. She had made it through safely. "*Thank you, Jesus, for not letting me choke and drown in the water,*" she prayed, suddenly feeling close to tears.

But she blinked them away and got to work. "*I knew you'd help me.*"

She laid the underpants on a chair. Then, taking up the dress, she worked her way into it, having to pull it over her wet head. As she expected, the bareness and cold underneath the dress felt terrible. She had to shiver as she sat down to put on her shoes and socks. The pale blue skirt still stuck out nicely around her, and, except for her stringy, wet hair, she was fairly satisfied with how she looked.

She gave the panties a last squeeze into the towel, then carried them with her as she hurried back through the Sunday School rooms. The staircase going down seemed steeper than she remembered, forcing her to go carefully.

Then, at the bottom, she opened the heavy door to the outside, and slipped silently out into the near-darkness. Past the church she crept, and into the parking lot. She knew approximately where her mother had parked, but still had to search through cars before finding their old, brown Chev.

Suddenly, the streetlight went on, flooding the parking lot with light! It startled her so that she dropped, huddling between two cars with her heart pounding. But the night stayed quiet: no one was walking around. Opening the car to the backseat, she threw the panties in, and closed the door again softly.

Then, back at the church and feeling even barer below in the night air, she was glad to get inside. She stepped into warmth, roast beef smell, and—music! The service had already started!

The congregation was singing, "Ju-ust as…I a-am witho-out one plea…." It was one of her favorite hymns, reminding her of the picture of Jesus opening his arms wide to suffer the little children. "Oh Lamb…of Go-od, I come…I…come."

She spied her mother and Carol seated at a nearby table; her mother's arm was raised to catch her eye. She stepped forward. *Here I come, Jesus. Just as I am.*

THE CAT'S TEETH

It was late in the days of the full moon, and by the time Laney Mahler had washed the supper dishes and could leave the house, the moon was already high in the sky. She hurried out the back door and around the house to the front to see if moonlight had reached the metal roof of the Angelos' barn.

It had. She knew it in advance, running through the house's shadow, knew it by the bright light ahead in the front yard. Then she saw the barn roof itself, aglow with silvery light so bright that it dimmed the hazy, starry sky.

Laney gave the secret whistle, blowing skillfully into her two cupped hands: "Woo-a-woo-woo-a!" She had walked a short way up the dirt road when, from further ahead, came the soft answer: "Woo-a-woo-a-woo-o."

Soon she saw Jenny Weimer's sturdy figure moving past the barn, the moon overhead casting her shortened shadow on the bottom of the wall. Laney started running toward her, awkwardly, both hands in her pants pockets. The two twelve-year-olds met quietly, grinning.

"I see you got out of piano practice," Jenny said.

"Yeah, just!" said Laney. "I finished the dishes and snuck out the back door." Turning around, they started back toward Laney's house, looming large in the moonlight. Ahead of them, below the road, lay the Mahlers' broad, shadowy field. "Isn't it a great night? I think this is the brightest moonlight I've ever seen."

"It's the kind of moon we had last Halloween."

"You're right." Laney chuckled. "That's one Halloween I'll never forget, 'specially the parade that night. You in that old, fake horse's head. Jackass Jenny."

"God, yes! You're supposed to say it all, though: Fat ass, Jackass Jenny." Jenny started laughing, and let it get loud. Laney loved her, once again, for her amazing ability to laugh at herself. "And you with that crazy tail people kept stepping on! Low-down, Lizard Laney!"

"That's me, Low-down Liz. It started out to be a dragon, you know."

"I was amazed your mom let you cut up that bedspread."

"That old green rag? She was glad to get rid of it, so she could buy a new one. And it was perfect. I made a good lizard,

I thought, except the head kept drooping over my face." Laney laughed and tripped over a stone.

"Watch out, goof."

"You were the one, though, Jen. You were a great jackass, kicking and wagging your big rear end around."

"My rear end? My big fat ass! Say it, Laney. A-s-s, Ass! Go on, say it!"

"Oh, shush. All right, ass. Your big fat ass." Then she had to laugh again, and the night became stranger and more wonderful. "Hey, let's walk through the field clear down to the river!"

"Why? It's dark as heck down there."

"No, it's not. Look at the moonlight on the meadow."

"Oh, you're right. It's so romantic. Mo-o-onlight—on the mea-do-o-w," Jenny sang in a loud and surprisingly good voice.

"Sh-h-h! Not so loud, Jackass! Somebody could hear you!"

"You're chicken, Low-down. Who could possibly hear us?"

But they quieted and stepped more softly, glancing around as the possibility dawned that they weren't necessarily alone in the night. After turning into the Mahlers' driveway, they crossed a strip of lawn, then picked their way down a gentle slope into the field. Silence lay in the lower air like something cool and solid. No wind whispered, no crickets chirped, no frogs sang down by the river. A thin cloud had drifted past the moon, and the world seemed to change.

"Look at the humps of weeds above the grass," Jenny muttered. "They look like bent-over bodies."

"Now who's chicken," Laney said. Straight ahead of them, across the field, lay Daugherty Creek. Laney, turning left, started on a curving trajectory toward the wider, slow-moving Kingman river. "C'mon, it's alright. It's still beautiful. It's a strange and beautiful kind of night."

"Weird, I'd say. It's a night for us to do something weird. What can we do?"

"Well, for a start," said Laney, "let's go see how the river looks in the moonlight. We'll have to watch out for jagger bushes. I know they're in here, somewhere. We'll try to skirt around them."

"Look at the dark line of ghosts over there."

"Elderberry bushes, ninny. My mom makes jelly out of them. But another problem is going to be mud, close to the water. There are swampy places. Not till you reach the willows, though, I think."

"We oughta make a map of this field." Jenny reached to finger a silvery milkweed pod in passing.

"Right. At least, mark a safe trail between the mud and the…. Uh-oh! Look out for that! I think—it is! It's a jagger bush!" Laney held her wrist high, backing away from the stinging nettle.

"I knew it. We're gonna run into more of 'em now," Jenny muttered, checking around for more of the deadly, jagged-edged leaves. "This strikes me as a bad omen. Someone or something doesn't want us coming down here."

"You and your omens! Ow, blast it! It hurts like fire." She rocked and moaned, gripping her wrist. "Let's go on, darn it, but watch our step!" They moved on cautiously through higher weeds. The field, in bright moonlight again, shortened before them as they neared shadowy trees that lined the river's edge.

"Uh-oh, the grass here feels wet," Jenny said. "We aren't getting into river water yet, are we?"

"No, silly. It never comes up here unless it's flooded. This is just dew. *Darn* it, this thing hurts!" Laney shook her whole arm.

"For God's sake," Jenny grumbled, "just say 'damn.'"

"Look at that patch of light—something's shining there in the grass."

Jenny moved toward it, and leaning closer to look, gave it a sharp kick. "It's a metal can." She bent down, picked it up, and laughed. "It's a coffee can! Hey, look, it even still has it's lid on. And it smells good! Now this is magic, Low-down! Now we're gonna have some fun! What can we do with this treasure?"

"Well, keep it, at least. We'll find some use for it." Laney paused to look around. "I think we'd better move to the right, toward the taller trees. There ought to be mud starting about now. That ugly orange stuff the river makes."

The Kingman River was orangish, especially when the water was low. People called it a sulfur river, and blamed the color on mines upstream. While they crept on, light above them had gradually dimmed, as the land sloped toward the river into a dark gloom that had gathered in the willows.

"I don't think the river's gonna be a glorious sight," said Jenny. "It's getting too dark to even see it. Uh-oh, I just stepped on something weird." Stooping in high grass, she came up with something that dangled from her hands. "Oh, my God!" she yelled.

"What?"

"It's a dead body! Ugh!" Dropping it quickly, she shook her wet hands.

"It looked like a skeleton," said Laney. "It won't hurt you. It's dead, silly."

"You can have it! I'm getting outta here!"

"Oh, Jackass, don't be such a ninny. I'm not afraid of it." Laney plodded through the grass, stooped, and gently lifted a small bundle of bones. "Look," she murmured. "It comes all apart. These little tiny things are ribs."

Jenny crept back. "What is it? A dog?" She moved closer.

"I can't tell. Maybe…."

Suddenly, Jenny bent down near Laney, then came up with something round and smooth. "Oh, hell, I think I've found the head!" She threw it back down. "Yuck!"

"Let me see it!" Laney said. She retrieved it and held it up, trying to find better light. "I believe it's a cat," she breathed. "Must be, with such a little nose. Poor thing. Look at the sharp little teeth. They're still in the skull."

Jenny, finding new courage, reached out to touch them. "Hey, they wiggle. Oops. Look, one of them came out!"

"Oh, boy! Let's carry this thing up into the moonlight, so we can see it better," said Laney.

They hurried a few steps up the slope to better light. There, in a state of pure wonder, they carefully extracted each tiny tooth, until Jenny held a small handful.

"Let me hold 'em, too," Laney said, and they transferred the teeth to her as carefully as if they were gems.

"Hey! We've still got the coffee can!" Jenny retraced her steps to lift it from the grass.

"I told you we'd find a good use for it!"

They deposited the teeth and clamped on the lid.

Then Jenny shook the can, which rattled so loudly, it startled them both. "Jeez, Louise!" She laughed and shook it some more. Setting up a rhythm, she started moving her rounded body to the beat.

"Quiet, Jackass! You'll wake the dead!"

"Ha ha! Maybe we'll wake the cat. He can't hurt us, though, without his teeth."

"Maybe he'll come *back* for his teeth," said Laney. "Maybe he'll come back to get even with us!"

"Let's dance, Low-down! Look, the light's a little brighter here!"

"You're a crazy loon, Jackass!" But Laney laughed and joined her, waving her arms to the rattling beat and swiveling her thin hips.

"Yay! Look at me! I got your teeth, you mangy cat! I'm Fat Ass Jackass Jenny!" Shaking the can toward the sky, she threw her wagging head into the dance.

"I'm Low-Down Liz," Laney sang out in what she thought was a southern drawl. "Worst Liz there is." She swayed with her arms overhead.

But they soon tired of this, and tapered off dancing. In the sudden quiet, dark and coolness descended heavily around them again. Stepping lower, they returned to the shadow of the trees, where thin branches curved and meandered like long, spidery arms. Ahead, in the slightly sulphur-smelling blackness, lay water. They could almost feel its presence.

"Maybe," said Jenny softly, "we should forget the river and go home."

Laney thought it over. Glancing around through the limbs, she studied a nearby trunk. "Let's hide the can in that hole in the tree, and get out of here."

"Good," Jenny said, handing her the can.

"This'll be a safe hiding place." Laney tucked it firmly into the hole. "It's above high water, I think."

"We gotta remember this spot, so we can find it again," Jenny said. "Next full moon, maybe we'll come back."

"Right. At least, on Halloween."

But the joy and enthusiasm were gone as they took a few careful steps, looking for an easy path back uphill "Oh, no. Damn! I just stepped in mud," Jenny muttered. "Which way do we go?"

"Well," Laney said, "I think to our right, past that broken trunk. But I'm not sure…. Hey! Turn around and look straight back, through here! What do you see?"

"It's water!" Jenny said. "Right here! God, it's scary! I didn't think it was so close!"

Stepping cautiously forward on spongy ground, they saw a thin line of light on dark water. Beyond it was blackness, then a broad stretch of water that shone with surprising light. All slowly, slowly moving. It was mesmerizing.

"I could actually lose my balance," said Laney.

"Well, don't. I just stepped in mud again, and it's deeper here. Oh, help." Trying to find firmer ground, Jenny had been forced to take more steps to keep her balance. "I'm in the damn mud here, Laney! Oops! This is that infernal cat's doing! I bet he was one of them orange cats."

"What?"

"I'm stuck, Laney! What can I do?"

"Well, stand still, Jackass. Quit jerking around, and quit yelling." Laney took splashing steps toward her. "I'm in the water now! It's up to my ankles!"

"I'm gonna try to take one big step backward," said Jenny.

"Watch out! There's mud here, too. It sucks at my feet!"

Suddenly, the brush behind them thrashed wildly with snapping, breaking branches. The girls froze in terror, standing hunched and off-balance. Dimly, a human head and shoulders emerged from the darkness.

"Hey, there, li'l gels," came a man's thin voice. "Wha's a matter? Got yourselfs in trouble, did you?"

Then more horror, a closer crunching of brush. The tall, thin man worked his way forward until his top half was in moonlight, revealing overalls and long, dangling arms.

Through her fright, Laney thought she recognized him. "Billy! Is it you? I know you. Do you remember me?" Her words came out high-pitched and frightened. She had seen him occasionally throughout her life—a tall, childlike man, made unforgettable once by rubbing her cheeks on his rough, stubbly chin.

"Who is he?" Jenny whispered hoarsely.

"Waaal," the peculiar, twangy voice answered, "one o' you is likely Harv Mahler's gel. Not the older one, Carol. Prob'ly his younges' one."

"That's right, Billy, Carol's at home tonight. I'm Laney." Thankfully, her voice had smoothed out. "This is Jenny Weimer. Steve and Mary's girl."

"Hmm. I don' know them well. But I know you oughtn't be out here in the dark. I seen you yellin' and jumpin' around like crazy. Dancin', weren't ya? I wished I could'a joined you!" He gave a cackling laugh, in enough light that the girls saw his mouth in a wide, toothless grin.

"We hafta go home!" Jenny sounded close to tears.

"We were just playing in the moonlight," Laney tried to explain, "and then we thought we'd take a look at the river."

"Waal, it ain't much to see, is it? I see youse're stuck in the mud. Gotta be careful, they's quicksand in places."

"We're okay," Laney said calmly. "We're on our way out now. We'll be heading for home." She tried to make it sound like a certainty. Nothing worse was going to happen.

"I like all you li'l gels." Billy was still grinning, moving a small branch aside to step closer. "I used to reach across the fence an' try to hug you Mahler gels. But you wouldn' let me get close, though. I never would'a hurt you, o' course."

"I remember, Billy. My mom and dad always liked you." Laney tried a sideways step, finding only deeper water. "But it's getting late, and we gotta go. Next our parents will be out looking for us."

"That's right!" Jenny agreed quickly. "They'll probably be showing up any minute." Attempting to move faster, she plunged hands first into the water. "Help, I'm drowning!" She came up sputtering.

"Dear God," Laney murmured, inching toward her as Jenny, upright again, took splashing steps toward the shore.

"Wait, you're headin' toward quicksand, goin' 'at way. Hol' still, an' I'll carry you to dry land." Billy broke through brush, moving toward Jenny.

But Jenny plowed on, calling back, "It's better over here, Laney!"

Laney stepped toward her through shallower water.

"Lemme hep you gels! It's nothin' for me to carry li'l persons like yourselfs. I'd hold you nice and easy." Billy maneuevered toward Laney, but she had pushed on and eluded him, stumbling and crashing her way after Jenny toward the tall weeds.

"Thanks, Billy," Laney puffed. "But we can do it ourselves. Thanks, though."

The man stood still then, watching them. Laney, daring a glance back, saw disappointment and sorrow in his shining eyes.

"You know, I could'a hepped you. But you're not lettin' me. Scared o' me, I guess."

The girls left him there, standing in the trees, in such deep dusk that when they looked back again, they couldn't see him. Hurrying through the brushy weeds, they reached higher ground and ran faster in the open. Brighter moonlight there seemed to them almost daylight as they angled toward the Mahler's chicken house, which was closer than the house. They crawled between barbed wires, scrambled up the slope and ran through apple trees, aiming for the back porch. Finally there, they stopped, wet and exhausted.

Jenny panted hoarsely, close to tears. "I've never been so scared in my life! I'm so damn glad to be up here where it's safe." She snuffled loudly. "Are you okay, Laney? My God, I can't believe what happened!"

"Me too, Jenny, I was scared out of my wits." She was watching the field behind them. "Whew! I can't talk!" Then, after expelling a deep breath, she said, "Honestly, though, I don't really think he'd have hurt us."

"What? You complete idiot! That's the kind of thinking that gets girls ravished, and murdered! He wanted to *carry* us, for cripe's sake!"

"He's like a big kid, Jenny. He may even be younger than we are, mentally. I've known him all my life, off and on. He's always been like that."

"Well, my dad'll call the police when I tell—"

"No, no! Don't tell your folks! Let's not tell anyone! Want to get our parents caught up in a lawsuit, or a court case, or something? They'd be so mortified, and it would ruin our names forever! Besides, we can't say that he hurt us, when he didn't."

Jenny hugged her arms and shivered while she thought. "Well, what'll we tell our parents, then? My whole front's wet, and I got this hideous mud all over my pants and shoes."

"Let's tell the truth, but leave Billy out of it. We went down to see the river, got into mud, and more or less fell in. Okay?"

"Okay, I guess. But, Laney?"

"What?"

Jenny's eyes shone with a new anxiety.

"*What?*" Laney repeated.

Jenny muttered intensely, "Remember what we were doing, before? This guy had no teeth. *Do you think the cat came back?*"

Laney stood straighter, thunderstruck. "Jenny! That gives me chills! What a horrible thought!"

"You said yourself he might come back after us, for what we did."

Laney turned to stare back toward the river. Then she gazed up at the shadowy house as if bewildered. Finally, she sagged. "Well, that's nonsense. Let's not start thinking up scary stuff. Maybe I'd better walk you home."

"What for? You'd have to walk back by yourself. I'll make it home. I'll *run,* not walk." But she glanced warily back over the field.

"Well," Laney sighed. "All I know is, I gotta pee and I'm going in. Do you want to come in and use our bathroom, quick? You can clean up a little. Do you have to pee, too?"

"Not anymore, I don't," Jenny said.

But there was no laughing as the girls said goodbye quietly, and parted for the night.

THERE'S LIKING
AND THERE'S LOVE

When Laney Mahler was fourteen, she broke a large front tooth in half, lying on her bed swinging the overhead light cord until the globe dropped from the ceiling and landed on her mouth. The next day, talking as little as possible because cold air hurt the tooth, she had to play for two funerals, the first on her own church's organ, the second on another church's piano. With her broken tooth hurting steadily, the quiet sobbing and grief at the funerals saddened her more than usual. After the second funeral she walked home in the rain. Home at last, she used what felt like the last of her energy clumping up the back porch steps.

"How'd it go, Honey?" her mother asked. "Oh, my gosh, you're soaked! I never thought to send you with an umbrella!" Bustling away in her self-blame, she took Laney's wet music case and set it on the linoleum by the door.

"This was the worst day of my life," Laney said. Taking a hand towel, she dried her face and drenched hair.

"You'd think someone from the church would've driven you home!"

"Everyone was going out to the cemetery afterwards, and I didn't want to stick around. So I came home." She laid the towel aside, then touched her fingers to her sore mouth. "I need a couple aspirins." Her mother hurried off for the aspirins.

Shortly after this day, Laney had painful dental work done, which resulted in a crown larger than the original tooth and slightly protruding. During the past year she'd been found to be nearsighted, and started wearing glasses. Meanwhile, her mother, trying to deal with Laney's fine, straight hair, had discovered home permanents. In her careful, thorough way, she always produced curl that was too tight and prone to be fuzzy. As the permanent grew out, it looked better, but then it was soon time for another permanent. Laney's older sister, Carol, who had just started nurse's training, had beautiful, naturally curly hair, and the unfairness of this had not escaped Laney's attention.

Already self-conscious with her new glasses, and unhappy with her hair, Laney became reluctant to smile because of the fat crown. She became a quieter girl, and less confident.

Intent on her studies and music for the church, her quietude reached a point where her mother told her she didn't seem to laugh much anymore.

Then, one day, the boy who sat behind her in eighth-grade homeroom started playing with her hair. Feeling the gentle tugging, she guessed that he was trying to curl a lock around his finger. She was annoyed, largely because she was embarrassed about the frizziness. Sometimes she moved her head to shake him off, but eventually he returned. Finally she started pretending indifference.

Until now, she had hardly noticed the boy. His name was Jimmy Bowman. About her height, he had anxious-looking brown eyes and crew-cut hair slicked down with some shiny product, from which a few sprigs escaped and stuck out.

One Saturday, Jimmy started riding his bike back and forth on the road in front of Laney's house. The first time she saw him whizzing by she thought it might be Jimmy, but he went so fast, she couldn't be sure. Soon afterward, on his return trip, she recognized the crew cut. He rode standing up, pedaling hard and bent over the handlebars like a racer. As she watched him through the lace curtain, her mother appeared at her shoulder.

"Who is that, I wonder."

"He's a boy from my homeroom at school. He sits right behind me."

"Ahah! You have an admirer," Vera said, laughing.

"Oh, Mom! We don't even talk. He lives out of town somewhere. I don't know what he's doing down here."

"You're not interested in him, then?"

"No! I hardly know him. He's not good-looking. Besides, I think he's younger than me."

"Look, here he comes again! Why does he have to pedal so hard? If he's hoping to see you, he shouldn't go so fast."

"Mom, get back, please! Don't move the curtains!"

Her mother stepped back and straightened the lace panel, now that he was past. "So, you have a boyfriend already, at fourteen."

"I do not! If I had one, it wouldn't be him. He's kind of sweaty and nervous-looking. And I told you he's too young." She turned away and returned to her Saturday job, cleaning the kitchen. But the bicycle parade continued for a while, with her mother returning to the window to chuckle. Laney became so annoyed with her, she came close to sympathizing with the boy.

In school Monday, there came a new development. That afternoon, as she was gathering her books to take home, Jimmy brushed roughly past, leaving on her desk a tiny, much-folded paper note. He continued on smoothly to the door, glancing around nonchalantly in case anyone was watching. Laney picked up the note wonderingly, then thrust it into a pocket.

She lingered over her books, giving Jimmy time to reach his bus before she went outside. In the hall, she decided to read the note before joining her friend Jenny, so she slipped into the girls' bathroom. She entered a stall, closed the door and sat down to rest her books on her lap.

"Dear Laney, you are the prettiest girl in the school. I love your beautiful brown eyes. Will you go to the movies with me this Saturday night? There's a good one coming at the Warner. Meet me outside tomorrow after school. Love, Jimmy."

Dear God, she thought, love? But, she had a date. Was it for real? She read the note again. Yes! Gradually she became excited. Even though it was with Jimmy. She refolded the note carefully, and returned it to her pocket. Hurrying outside, she tried to see him in a different light. With some surprise, she was succeeding. He was a boy, wasn't he? He wasn't all that bad. And he'd asked her for a date!

Seeing Jenny waiting on the sidewalk, Laney made a sudden decision not to tell her. Jenny would laugh that loud laugh of hers. She decided to keep the note secret from any of the girls. As she and Jenny walked home together, Laney managed to keep her voice calm, but Jenny had to ask her twice not to walk so fast.

Arriving home, Laney steeled herself to tell her mother. She set her books on the kitchen table, deciding to tell her right away.

Her mother, who came to meet her, responded to the news with shock. For a few long seconds, she actually seemed to grow paler. "A date. So he's serious. You're too young for this, Elaine. Carol had her first date her senior year." Then she pondered it, staring into space. "Still…you're fourteen. But you don't like this boy."

"He's not a bad kid, Mom. At least, he's not one of the loud, moron types."

"So, he's Jimmy, you said? Jimmy who?"

"Jimmy Bowman."

"Hmm. I wonder if he could be the grandson of old Nate Bowman, at the bank."

"I have no idea."

Her mother thought further. "Do you want to go? Your dad probably won't like it, you know. He might put his foot down."

"I think I would like to go. It's exciting to have a date, Mom. What I can't figure out is why he's interested in me. I look so awful."

"Now, stop that. You have a nice face. Your perm will soon grow out."

"Well." Laney sighed. "Will you ask Dad, then?"

"Yes. I'll talk to him about it when he gets home tonight."

That evening, Laney was nervously practicing on the piano when she heard her dad's footsteps climbing the back porch stairs. She played more softly, trying to listen to the conversation in the kitchen. Finally her dad's weary voice rose. "Judas Priest!" It was the one swear word he allowed himself, and it shook her so that her fingers stumbled on the keys. Then, having nearly stopped playing, she resumed her normal pace. The kitchen voices softened to serious talk, mostly from her mother. Finally they became quiet.

In homeroom the next day, Laney and Jimmy avoided each other's eyes. When school was over, Laney gathered her books slowly to let him leave ahead of her. Then she walked outside, where she found him waiting at the end of the wide porch. She walked straight to him, hoping none of her friends were watching. "Thanks for the invitation, Jimmy. Yes, I'd like to go."

His face froze for a second. "You would? Great!" He gave a short, startled-sounding laugh. "Well, that's great. Which movie do you want to see? The Strand has one about a horse, and the Warner has a comedy. Take your pick."

Laney, rattled to be given a choice, managed to say the comedy at the Warner sounded good.

Jimmy said that was great with him. "My dad has to drive me," he said, "'cause it's too far to walk. Can you get there yourself?"

"Yes. It's too far for me to walk, too. My dad will likely drive me."

"It starts at seven, so let's meet there a little before, about a quarter till. If we're early we can get a good seat. It might be crowded, you know. Saturday night."

Laney agreed. Then they parted, Jimmy heading off at great speed to meet his bus. Laney took the three steps to the sidewalk thinking with mild shock that it was now an accomplished thing. The date was locked in, and there'd be no getting out of it. She had to walk a few slow steps to get her racing heart to settle down.

The next few days, she and Jimmy passed each other in school without a word. Meanwhile, her earlier exultation faded as the doubt and fright beneath it rose to the surface. What would they talk about? She knew nothing about him! What if they had to sit together in the dark before the movie started? Would he expect her to hold hands? She saw now that she'd made a rash mistake, accepting the date mainly because she was flattered to be asked. But she couldn't confide her dread to her parents for fear they'd make her call it off, which would be so humiliating it was unthinkable.

Her mother, watching her, tried to be encouraging. But her dad, to whom her mother had shown the note, grew cross. In a sour tone, he reminded her that her eyes weren't even brown, they were hazel, almost green. Laney found herself caught between agreeing with her father and defending Jimmy. So she suffered in silence.

Saturday evening she climbed into the brown, '39 Chev beside her dad for the drive to the Warner. He parked in the theater's small parking lot, where they sat in the car and looked around. Apparently they were the first to arrive.

In the last couple days Laney's father had seemed to get over his irritation, becoming almost sympathetic. Taking a look over at her, he said, "Buck up, now. It can't be as bad as you think."

She laughed shakily, nodding.

They sat a couple minutes longer, then Laney thought Jimmy and his father might also be waiting in their car, so they climbed out. They stood below the Warner's marquee, where the wait lengthened to ten minutes. It was five minutes to seven. Laney was starting to sweat. Where were they? They were late! Of all the horrors she had imagined, this was a new one.

"Is it possible they could have gone to the Strand?" her father asked.

"Jimmy was so clear about it," she insisted. "We decided on the Warner because there's a comedy here, and we both chose the comedy."

But a minute later she was clinging to the car seat as her dad drove swiftly, for him, heading for the Strand. When they got there, he stopped in front of the theater to let her out while he parked. There seemed no one waiting outside, just people entering the theater. Laney darted left and right, searching, until her dad joined her. Together they gazed around in the marquee's bright light.

"Well," he asked, "what now?" His lit face, sun-reddened below the white brow, began to look worried. "Do you want to step inside, and look around for him?"

"I don't know what to do," she said, guarding against tears.

"Let's go back," he said. They piled back into the car for another wild ride back to the Warner. The parking lot now was nearly full, so Laney climbed out and her dad drove into the lot.

There they were, Jimmy and a tall man wearing what Laney thought of as Sunday clothes, a dark suit and a white shirt. He removed a cigarette from his mouth, dropped it, and blew roughly through his lips. As Laney's dad approached, a shorter, tired-looking man in his work clothes, the taller man's face looked smug. "Well, look who's here. Are these the folks you told me about, Jimmy? A little late, aren't they?"

Jimmie, peering around from behind him, said nothing.

"This is my father," Laney said, as her dad stepped forward with a hand starting to reach out. The other man looked at the hand and ignored it.

"We were here at a quarter till seven," her dad said. "That was the plan, I believe."

"Well, now, that can't be right, can it? We were here then, weren't we, Jimmy?"

Laney heard words burst from her mouth. "We waited here so long, we drove over to the Strand to see if you had gone there."

"I thought so! Just like I told you, Jimmy. We came here, and they went to the Strand." He gave an amused chuckle, shaking his head. "And now it's too late, the show's already started."

Jimmy, frowning anxiously, pushed forward. "Hello, Mr. Mahler."

"This is Jimmy, Dad," Laney said.

"I'm glad you're here!" the boy said. "Come on, Laney, let's go in! It's not too late, Dad. They're probably showing previews." He took Laney's hand and drew her toward the entrance. "Look, I already got the tickets."

Laney glanced back at her father, who stood stiffly erect and looked furious. Jimmy's father was turning to go, cupping a hand to light a new cigarette.

Inside the theater, Jimmy lead her down the dark aisle and found two empty seats. Previews were playing. As he released her hand she seated herself, thinking dazedly that holding hands was nothing to worry about.

The main feature was beginning as Jimmy leaned his head toward her and said quietly, "Sorry about my dad."

"It's okay," was all she could say.

"I call him Dad, but he's my stepdad. He's…well, anyway. We must have got here about the time you left for the Strand."

"Oh. Well, it's all right, Jimmy. Thanks for telling me that."

He nodded and fell silent. Laney, imagining having a stepfather like Jimmy's, turned enough to look at his face. He met her eyes, in the near darkness, and she faced front again.

He leaned closer, whispering, "Don't worry about me. He isn't always like that." Then he settled back, took in a breath that lifted his shoulders, and let it out again.

Laney sat staring straight ahead but absorbing nothing that was happening on the screen.

In a short time, the movie took hold of them. Jimmy started laughing beside her, and Laney finally laughed out loud. A small release at first, but soon she let herself go completely. As the story's characters became embroiled in a hilariously impossible situation, they both rocked with laughter.

When the movie ended and the lights went on, people around them still chuckled as they rose to leave. The two of them shuffled up the aisle together. Jimmy took her elbow, and once again, it felt just natural.

As they stepped outside, Laney's dad was waiting near the door. They joined him as Jimmy's dad approached from the car lot.

"Dad," Jimmy said, "I want to talk to Laney."

"You've had all night to do that. I'm tired of waiting. Let's go home."

"Can't I just have a minute?"

"Get in the car!"

"Good night, Jimmy!" Laney called hastily as the boy stepped backwards, following his father. "I had a good time."

"So did I, Laney. Thanks for coming...." A wave of his hand, and he faded into the darkness of the parking lot.

As Laney and her dad reached their car, a new Oldsmobile roared past them, gleaming in the lights from the theater.

Laney's father started the car as she climbed in. He was fuming. "I'd like to knock the daylights out of him! He's a liar, and he made me feel like two cents."

"I know, Dad. Jimmy said he's not his real dad, he's his stepdad. I don't think he cares much for Jimmy. Did you hear what he told him just now? *Get in the car!* In front of us! And Jimmy has to live with that."

Her dad pondered it, shaking his head. "Well, that's a shame. I'm sorry for the boy. But don't ask me to drive you to meet him again, Laney. I'm sorry, but...." He sighed. "I'm not about to go through that again."

"Oh, Dad...." Gloom settled in the car as they drove past the few streetlights, turning south toward the bridge. "And I had such a good time tonight."

"Really? Well, that's a surprise."

"I know! I never thought I would enjoy myself so much. Jimmy's a nice guy. It was a great movie, and we laughed our heads off. It was actually fun."

Her father cast her a long look. Then they rode in silence while the car bumped over the wooden planks of the Daugherty Creek bridge. A short distance ahead, their house rose dimly above the intervening field, with a light shining in the kitchen window.

"Dad," Laney said thoughtfully, "Something else. When Jimmy told me about his stepdad, I was feeling really bad. And he told me not to worry about *him*, because the man wasn't always like that. Imagine! You know he *is* always like that. Jimmy said it to comfort *me*!"

Her father said under his breath, "Judas Priest." He drove slowly into their driveway, stopped before the garage, and remained seated. Laney waited with him, looking out at the peaceful night.

"Well," he said, "if you really had a good time tonight, and if he asks you out again, I guess I'd be able to take you."

Laney fell silent. She began to feel choked. Tears were springing to her eyes, and her throat constricted so tightly, she could hardly breathe. She tried to calm herself, because she needed to speak.

Still trying to prepare herself, she climbed out and walked around the front of the car. But tears were running down and they were nearing the steps. It couldn't wait; she had to speak *now. Get it out!*

"Dad," she said with her voice squeezed high and tearful, "I just…." She forced it out. "I just want to thank you. For everything."

He almost stopped beside her, then touched her shoulder briefly as they started up the steps together. She knew that he also was struggling. He too wanted to say something, but just couldn't get past the embarrassment.

DAISY JAMES

Laney Mahler, at fifteen, had a clear memory of sitting on Daisy James's lap as a small child and touching her wrinkled, old face. She still remembered how soft it felt. Daisy's brown skin lay loosely over her facial bones, darker in the hollows. Her eyes were rather dull, but watchful. Her lips were heavy and finely shaped, the lower thrust slightly forward. But her feature that was most remarkable, to the Mahlers and other people in Plum Bottom, was her cap.

She was never seen without her cap, even in summer. Knitted from dark wool, she wore it drawn down over her ears. She also wore long skirts nearly to her ankles, and a shawl, or a man's long, drooping sweater. But that cap! Her head filled only the bottom of it, while the top rose above her head in a bulbous knob, positioned somewhat forward. Everyone who knew her was mystified as to what was in it.

Once when Laney was little, she had asked Daisy what was inside her cap, and had met with a stony silence. Laney's mother, Vera, had cautioned her never to mention the cap again. Between Vera and Daisy James stretched a bond of courtesy stronger than ordinary friendship.

On this May afternoon, it was Laney's little sister, Irene, aged three, who was sitting in Daisy's lap. Daisy and Reney, as they called Irene, sat together on the back porch rocker. Vera sat on the swing, peeling potatoes, and Laney was perched near them on the porch railing.

As Laney watched, Reney raised a pointing finger to touch Daisy's lips. Daisy laughed, hissing through her teeth, "Tsss, tsss, tsss". But Reney saw what she wanted to see—Daisy's little white wad of paraffin that she chewed for gum. Reney crowed in delight, and Vera laughed along with her, but Laney watched unsmiling. She was annoyed by Daisy's closeness with Reney.

Reney had half-moon eyes, their bottoms hidden by her rounded, laughing cheeks, and hair of blond silk that slipped through a barrette like butter. When she bobbed and soared and sang on her rocking horse, Vera said, "Wouldn't it be nice if she could stay like this forever?" The Mahlers were not very demonstrative, and Reney somehow uncorked them all; they poured out on her all the love that seemed bottled up from each other. The relationship was especially close between Reney and Laney. Ever since Reney was a baby, Laney was the one who best understood her childish babble, and read her storybooks to her until they were falling apart.

Now, as Laney watched, Reney's quick little hand reached down inside Daisy's "boo-sum", as Daisy called it, and drew out a small, round snuff box.

"Wha's that!" Daisy said in mock surprise. Vera scolded, embarrassed, but Daisy chuckled as she put the box back. Laney knew from long experience that Daisy also kept something else down there, something that looked like a tiny, crumpled sack. "She's just a chile," Daisy was saying, "she don' mean no harm."

Laney, finally irritated beyond endurance, slid down from the railing to leave. As her mother lifted questioning eyes, Laney sent her a look that she hoped conveyed her disapproval. Then she kept going, down the porch steps and across the short yard, heading for the field.

The Mahlers' land was bordered on two sides by water, on the north by Daugherty Creek, and on the west by the wider Kingman River. The whole area, which lay below the hills of the town, was called Plum Bottom. As a small child, never seeing that colloquial name in print, Laney had thought it meant *plumb* bottom, the very bottom. Not happy about living in the plumb bottom of the town, years later she was pleased to learn that the name came from wild plum trees that had once grown there, on the low, rolling plain.

Having crossed the field, Laney reached its northwest corner, where the creek and the river met. A concrete abutment there, shaped like a ship's bow, projected out into the waters—a spot Laney and Jenny called "the point". The clear, brown creek swept past on the right and the wider, orangish river glided by on the left. Beyond the point, the waters merged, their colors blending, to form a larger, more powerful river.

Sitting on the concrete with her feet hanging down, Laney watched the waters sweep past below, and waited until she thought Daisy must have gone home. Then, lingering in the river's bordering willow trees, she saw the old woman just leaving—starting out on her usual shortcut, through the field. Lately, Daisy had been taking Reney with her partway into the field, with Vera watching from the lawn above; now, Daisy stepped carefully down the sloping bank with Reney in tow.

As they strolled in the field, Daisy occasionally stooped to gather young dandelion greens for her supper. Then, turning with her armload of greens, she sent Reney home. The child trotted obediently back to her mother, with her golden curls bouncing.

Daisy watched and waved, then turned eastward in the field, to clamber up onto the road before it rose too high at the bridge.

A few days later, Laney and her friend Jenny walked home from school together, discussing the school year's end and final exams. When they reached the Mahlers' driveway, Jenny had a new thought.

"Hey," she said, "How come Daisy James is at your place all the time?"

"I don't know," Laney said with a shrug. "She's not there *all* the time."

"She's there almost every day. Mom says she and your mom are thick as thieves. What's she to you, anyway?"

Laney, irked, took a breath and answered smoothly, "When Mom and Dad first moved here, they didn't have a garden yet, and Daisy gave them a lot of vegetables. I don't remember it, of course. Mom said Daisy had a big garden then and a nicer house, too, when her husband was alive. His name was Clarence. They came from Jamaica."

"Jamaica? Hmm!" Jenny was impressed with this. She shifted her books to her other hip, wanting to talk.

But Laney started into the driveway. "I need to go in now and do my homework. I have to play for choir practice tonight. See you tomorrow."

———

The weather had been so warm and humid, people were saying that they had gone from winter directly into summer. Then one morning came the awaited rain—a heavy storm, with flashes of lightning and pounding, crackling thunder. The downpour continued, off and on, through the first night and the following day.

The third day, a Friday, it seemed tapering off, so Laney was given the job of taking a dozen eggs over to Andy Werner's store. In a late afternoon drizzle, she took an umbrella and started off toward the Daugherty Creek bridge.

Andy Werner sold what she and her older sister Carol considered the world's best penny candy. Today, with her mother's eggs and extra money, she planned to buy some peanut squares for Carol, Reney and herself, in addition to a couple items for her mother.

When she arrived at the store, the sky was darkening again, with a low rumble of thunder. She groaned inwardly as she grappled with her egg sack and umbrella at the door, then finally stepped into the warmth of the small, crowded room.

Laney had known Andy's store since she was Reney's age, when she and Carol had walked there bare-footed, stepping carefully over the bridge's floor boards to avoid splinters. The whole front end of the counter was still a secret delight to her, filled with penny candy. Around most of the room, the walls were lined with shelves containing everything from canned vegetables to motor oil. Stretching along the front wall, by the door, was a long bench for loafers.

Fat Joe Schwartz, night watchman at the sawmill, sat there today, beside Pat Murray, a coal miner with a high voice and a long, corded neck. Farther over sat a gaunt, elderly man Laney didn't know. In front of the counter stood a dark figure—Daisy. She was so soaking wet her cap drooped. Behind the counter, Andy bent his shining, bald head as he lifted eggs out of Daisy's cloth bag and into a box.

The men were grinning and whispering to each other as they watched this egg transaction. Then they grew quiet, and Laney suspected that it was because they had seen her egg sack. She grew hot inside her jacket, angry with Daisy for being there and putting her in the same category as she, another groveling egg-seller.

Having seen Laney come in, Daisy fixed her dark eyes on her. "'Lo, Laney. Some rain, ain't it?" Laney read in her shortened gaze that she was aware of the grinning men behind her.

Since Daisy took up most of the counter, Laney set her wet umbrella on the floor and held onto her egg sack. Then, one-handed, she worked awkwardly with her jacket zipper.

Daisy took salt and flour in trade, and counted out twenty-two cents for Andy from a small purse. Then she put her purchases in her cloth bag, tucked the bag under her shawl, and turned fully to face Laney. "What's 'a matter," she said flatly, "cat got your tongue?"

This time Laney couldn't pretend she hadn't heard her. Sweating, and with her heart pounding, she kept her eyes down and remained silent. After a bit Daisy swept past her and outside into the freshening rain.

Joe muttered, during the men's snickering, that Daisy was Andy's girlfriend.

"What?" Andy lifted his round head.

"I said, Daisy James is your girlfriend," Joe said louder, his plump face reddening.

Andy just sucked in his mouth, not wearing his upper teeth, but his eyes sharpened. Wordlessly he opened Laney's egg sack for a quick count. Then, with her eggs and Daisy's, he traveled to his little kitchen in back, hobbling on legs so bowed that he leaned left and right as he walked.

"Them skirts of hers weighs a ton," Joe said, nudging Pat Murray. "'Specially now, soaking wet."

Pat replied, "I heard she takes her bath in Daugherty Creek. Never takes her clothes off." He chuckled at his own wit.

The older man spoke up: "What I want to know is, what she keeps in that cap."

"She keeps her valuables up there, her diamonds and gold," said Joe. "Don't she, Andy?"

Andy, returning from the kitchen, pinched his mouth in tighter.

"She keeps her eggs up there till they get ripe," Pat intoned, "then she sells them to Andy. Remind me not to buy eggs from you, Andy. Ha Ha."

Andy looked thoughtful. Then he met Laney's eyes with a look that went straight to her guilty heart. "She doesn't have many hens," he said quietly, lisping slightly without his teeth. "She never has a whole dozen eggs. But she's careful, she don't keep 'em too long. They're always good and fresh."

Laney avoided his eyes. "I need Chase and Sanborn, drip grind," she muttered, "and a box of Duz." Candy was out of the question, now. She stood waiting while Andy loaded the items into a larger sack, took her money, and handed her change.

Then she hurried outside with her sack, and opened her umbrella in the blessed coolness of the rainy dusk.

She plodded slowly around puddles, wanting to make sure Daisy was well ahead of her. Soon she would have to pass the woman's small house, near the creek. As her beleaguered brain cleared a little, the thoughts came as sharp as arrows. What had she done? Why hadn't she spoken up for Daisy? Daisy, who'd loved her since she was a baby!

A gust of wind blew spray under her bobbing umbrella, and it seemed for a moment that Daisy was right in front of her, in the hissing, spitting rain. Yearning to get home, Laney kept her slow, deliberate pace, making sure she wouldn't pass Daisy's house until after Daisy had gone inside.

———— ✦ ————

All night, rain pattered on the roof above Carol's and Laney's bedrooms. Carol was there for the weekend, Harv having driven her home Friday night from the hospital in Cambria, where she was a student nurse.

When the two sisters arose Saturday morning, Carol said, "I'm going out the road today to check the bridge. I'll bet the water's getting close under the floorboards."

"I crossed it last night," Laney said, "but it was too dark and rainy to see the water. I could hear it rushing, though. Really fast."

When they went downstairs, they found their father standing with his bricklayer's arms folded, gazing out the kitchen window. Laney hurried to look out beside him.

The Kingman River, across the wide field, was normally too low to be seen. Today it was slightly visible, a flat line gleaming here and there behind the bordering trees. The water was rising, but appeared still below the trees.

From the window, they had a fairly good view of the field, as the house was built above a cellar and on higher ground. After days of heavy rain, the field occasionally flooded, and then it became a natural wonder. People from town drove down to the bridge to enjoy the view, when the field had become a lake, mirroring the Mahlers' house and outbuildings. When people asked Laney how they were faring down in Plum Bottom, she had a short, terse answer ready: they were high and dry.

Harv grumbled about his forced vacation. After a cold winter and wet spring, with few inside jobs, he needed to work. He stood around getting in the way as Laney cleared the breakfast dishes. Finally he took Reney down to the cellar, where the furnace room was his cozy retreat.

While Laney did her Saturday cleaning, she could hear them down there cracking hickory nuts. Tick, tick, *tock,* the nut usually breaking on the third hammer strike. Between these blows came Reney's muffled singsong and her dad's hushed, excited voice he kept just for her, "Look at *that* one!"

—⚬⚬⚬—

That afternoon, while Carol earned her usual dollar cleaning house for the Angelos, Laney and Jenny studied together at Jenny's house, conjugating Latin verbs, interspersed with their usual silliness and boy talk. It was after four o'clock when they looked out to see that the clouds were breaking up and the sun was shining.

"It's a wonder your field didn't flood," Jenny's mother said as Laney came downstairs, ready to leave.

"It still could, I guess," she replied, "but I doubt it. This morning Carol said the water at the bridge was halfway up the banks. Probably it's gone down some, by now."

Walking home, she happily inhaled the sweet, grassy smells of the sparkling day. She had just passed the Angelos' barn when, looking a distance ahead, she caught a bright gleam of sunlight on water. The part of the field she could see, just below the road, was flooded all the way to the bridge. She broke into a run to get past her house. Then, looking west, she saw the Kingman's water shining in its willow trees. Most of the field, in the center, was still above water.

She took it all in quickly, then hurried around the house and up the back porch steps for a better view. She saw that the low land before the point was all flooded. In a jarring moment, she imagined getting stuck out there, with water rising all around her. On the field's east side, below the bridge, she saw that Daugherty Creek and the water in the field were one.

Running into the kitchen, she looked for her mother, and immediately heard her footsteps thundering overhead. *Why would she be running?* Vera's feet continued down the stairs— then came a faltering step, after which she pounded faster down to the landing.

Laney rushed into the hallway, yelling, "What is it, Mom? Are you all right?"

Vera hobbled down from the landing, with wet hair hanging around her face. "Laney! Help me, I'm beside myself! Reney's gone! I can't find her!"

Laney stood straight and cool, her mind empty. "Well, isn't she up taking her nap?"

"She's gone from her bed, while I was in the tub! I'm crippled now, I just turned my ankle!" Moaning, she limped into the living room, and while Laney stood frozen, she searched behind the drapes, and opened the closet door to grope among the coats.

"What are you searching such dumb places for?"

"Go search the cellar! We've got to make sure she's not in the house, before we go outside!

"Well, I'd call her first."

"I've called and called! She doesn't answer, and she doesn't come!"

Laney studied this. "Where's Dad?"

"Took the car to get gas."

"He's got Reney with him then!"

Vera straightened behind the couch. "Without telling me? How could he have taken her and not told *me*?" Her voice broke, and fright rang through Laney like a bell.

Stepping back into the hall, Laney raised her voice, aiming to be heard throughout the house. "Reney! *Ree-neee*!" Silence. "Well, did you check my closet? She plays house in there."

"Yes, yes." Vera dropped abruptly onto a chair to grip her ankle. "I've searched everywhere upstairs. I'll search better in here, while you go down to the cellar. " She groaned. "Why did I have to hurt myself *now*? God help me!"

"This is craziness, she's with Dad!" Laney held exasperation around herself like a cloak as she ran down the cellar steps. Calling, she checked the dark potato bin, and under the shelves of canned fruit. She peered into the laundry tubs, and into the dirty coal bin where Reney never would have gone. In the heater room, she crept behind the furnace, and around it to the outside door: latched.

Then Harv's voice sounded upstairs. She ran through the cellar and bolted up the steps.

Her parents were in the kitchen, standing together. The news was written on her mother's face; she stood sobbing, one hand covering her mouth.

Laney drew a hoarse breath and started wailing.

"Stop it, Laney! Now, Vera, calm yourself." Harv, shorter than Vera, became their sharp-eyed strength. "She's around here someplace. What was she doing before her nap? Did she say anything when you put her down?"

"She asked about Daisy!" said Vera. "She asked if Daisy would come, now that the sun was shining."

Harv's face lost all expression as he turned to the kitchen window. The creek's water along the road had spread further west, covering about half the field, and the Kingman's shore area was covered. "I'll walk out into the field," he said. "You're positive she's not in the house?"

Laney assured him that they were.

Vera said tearfully that she'd better phone the Angelos and have Carol come home.

"Shouldn't someone run over to check on Daisy James?" asked Laney.

"You go!" called her dad from the porch. "Watch the field as you run past. If she's not at Daisy's, bring Daisy back with you."

"Harv, be careful! I don't know if you should go into that field!" Vera called. But he didn't answer, already down the steps and heading for the bank, with Laney hurrying after him.

Vera stood transfixed, watching them go. Then, left alone, she limped to the telephone to call the Angelos.

Laney's legs felt stiff as she ran down the driveway, but as she turned onto the road they loosened and she picked up speed, racing past water that glittered in the dazzling, late sun.

In the field to her left, her father strode, keeping an eye on the Kingman. "Reney! *Ree-neee*!" he called, his voice rising so calm and sweet that Laney's throat tightened, and she could hardly make a sound.

Crossing the bridge, she cured the problem and called, but her voice was nearly lost in the water's roar. Watching brush wobble past below, it struck her that Reney would have been afraid of such loud, rushing water. The realization struck her sharply that wherever Reney was, she was lost and terrified. "*Please, God, please, God,*" she prayed mindlessly, as she left the bridge and turned toward Daisy's small house.

Arriving there, she pounded on the door. "Open the door, Daisy! It's me, Laney!"

The door opened a crack, and one eye appeared. "What you want?"

"Is Reney in there? Do you have her, Daisy?"

The door opened wider. "Reney? How would I have her? I ain't seen her!"

Laney panted, dazed. "She's gone, disappeared from her bed! She was taking her nap! She asked about you, just before that! Now the field's flooded...."

She watched fear reach Daisy's eyes. The old woman stepped outside and seemed startled further to see the Daugherty sweep along near her house, carrying a leafy branch like a sail. "Git goin'! Git!"

Laney fell back as Daisy waved her out of the way, and in her long skirts and house slippers, set out running.

Laney started after her, and overtook her on the bridge. Looking ahead, she saw activity at the house. The police car sat in the driveway, and a car she didn't recognize. Carol was there, standing by Jenny's parents. People milled about, and Laney, running, searched for Jenny. She located her friend, already facing her. *Give me a sign*, she thought, but Jenny's arms remained at her sides.

When they met at the gate, Jenny looked stricken. "I can't believe this, Laney." Her fright reinforced the horror of the situation, and Laney burst out sobbing. Jenny cried along with her as, arm in arm, they ran stumbling together to join the crowd at the steps.

Officer Buck Schrock and Harv Mahler first tried to share command, until Harv let Buck assume it all. Buck assigned people places to search: the Mahlers' small barn, chicken house, smokehouse, corncrib, and garage, though Vera's stunned and defeated eyes suggested to Laney that these areas had already been searched.

People scattered and the property became strange, not the Mahlers' anymore, given over to neighbors and friends. From all around in the growing dusk, voices Reney didn't know rose calling her name.

Laney and Jenny searched the chicken house, scattering hens that had just climbed the roost. They squawked and ran, but stayed in the house, reluctant to go outside in the night. Laney lifted the heavy lid on the feed barrel to reach down into the darkness, and was struck by the futility of it all.

"Let's get out of here," Jenny yelled, and it was a relief to them both to run back to the house.

Mrs. Mahler stood with her head bent beside the preacher, who had arrived with other men from the church. One of them had brought along his daughter Carol's age, and she and Carol huddled together.

On the porch above, in the kitchen's light, Daisy sat in the rocking chair, rocking, rocking. Anger swelled in Laney, to think that Daisy wasn't trying to help.

She was about to shout at her, when suddenly Daisy called down, "She's trapped!"

"What?" Laney yelled up at her.

"She's trapped," Daisy called again, in a voice thick with tears. "Or she's stuck someplace, and can't get out. That she don't come home."

Bud Moser from church asked who she was, and Leo Angelo said, "Just a crazy old neighbor woman."

"She *ought* to feel bad," Laney shouted. "It's her fault! She's the one who taught Reney to go out into the field!"

"Shut up!" Carol grabbed Laney's arm and held it tightly as she dragged her away. "Leave it to you to open your big mouth."

"Shut up yourself!" Laney yanked her arm back. "I'm right! Reney'd never have gone out in that field, except for Daisy!"

"*Do you think Daisy doesn't know that?*" Carol hissed, eyes shining in her fury.

Laney opened her mouth again, but didn't speak.

Yes! the realization struck her. Of course! Daisy knew that, knew it better than anyone. But she'd had to shout those terrible words. She had really hurt Daisy this time.

"Daisy, I'm sorry!" Laney called up to her in a voice that was breaking. People milled around her, and she couldn't be sure Daisy had heard. "Please forgive me, Daisy!" she blubbered. "I'm so sorry! It isn't your fault, it isn't anybody's fault! I love you, Daisy. I've always loved you."

As she spoke, her dad was talking behind her, trying to persuade the men to wade out into the water. "Not in a straight line, but zigzagging, left and right. That way, we might come across her. We've got to find her, you know. Vera's got to know, or she'll have no peace."

The men avoided his shining eyes, and Laney knew why. The Kingman hovered on the brink; it was getting too dark to see; there weren't enough men, and they'd be too strung-out.

"We can't go out there, Harv." Jenny's dad finally spoke, a short, anxious man. "If the Kingman breaks through, it'll wipe out everything in its path! The river's current could set up and anything out there'd be drawn down the river."

"That's right," said Tom Shumaker, from the church, "her body'll likely be found somewhere downstream when the water goes down."

"Look out! There she goes!" Buck yelled, and Laney watched a spectacle she had never before witnessed. In light from the rising moon and the streetlight at the bridge, dark water was moving. It swept eastward from the Kingman toward the waiting lake. When the waters met, they seemed to swell slightly, forming waves that pushed on toward the road. Then the whole black spread of water rocked gently, and grew still.

Suddenly, Mrs. Mahler gave a cry, and Laney knew that Reney was gone and she would have to face it. Jenny reached around her shoulders trying to hug her. Laney pulled away and was starting toward her mother, when her dad brushed past her. For some reason, he was running down the driveway.

Then Laney saw beyond him, on the bank, a dark figure creeping down to the water. Then into the water. It was Daisy.

A man shouted, "What's she doing? Fool woman!"

And another, "You come outa there! We got trouble enough!"

"It's Daisy! Oh my God!" Vera swore, and then shouted, "Daisy, come back!"

But Daisy waded on, into water that suddenly deepened to her hips. Leaning forward and dragging her skirts, she was on her old course, straight into the field.

Laney came to as she saw her dad turning onto the road. "Daisy," she called, "come back! Please! Don't go out where it's deep!"

Daisy, in water to her waist, raised her arms to keep them free and plowed on, starting her slight angle toward the road.

Laney found her legs working beneath her, running and stumbling on the road as she tried to keep her eyes on Daisy. Stronger runners were overtaking her, first Leo, then Buck and another man. Then a car passed them all, and inside the rear window, she glimpsed her mother.

Daisy was farther ahead, the water swallowing her until Laney could barely see her head. Then she realized Daisy was close enough the creek that she was feeling it's pull downstream.

Laney had nearly reached the bridge when she saw Daisy go under. A few terrible seconds passed, and then she re-emerged, with one hand clutching her cap and the other trying to reach the rock wall.

Along the road before the bridge stretched a wire fence, and Harv was bending the top down, trying to get a leg over. Laney reached his side, and looked straight down to see Daisy. She was grabbing for handholds on the rock wall, fighting the current, while beside her, water splashed and swirled against the concrete abutment.

Harv made it over the fence, and stood on the narrow strip of land. Then he lay down flat atop the wall and reached an arm down toward Daisy. But, as the assembled runners watched, she slipped silently into the water. Then she was gone.

Harv stood up straight, faced the water, and jumped. "Be careful!" Leo shouted.

From near them under the bridge came a cry, thin as night wind.

Leo next scrambled over the fence and jumped in, throwing up spray; then Buck jumped in after him.

Laney leaned over the fence watching through long seconds. Then a figure appeared from under the bridge, barely above the roiling water. It was Daisy, one hand clinging to the wall. Two heads. Laney was confused; both heads looked small and pale.

The three men in the water formed a chain, all gripping the rocks. Reney's frightened cry floated over the water, sweet and clear. Harv took her from Daisy, her thin arm shining white as she clung around his neck. With agonizing slowness, Harv passed her carefully to Buck, and then Buck passed her to Leo.

At last she was held up to the waiting Bud Moser, who knelt atop the wall near Vera's reaching arms.

Relief shivered through Laney, hinting at the possibility of normal life. A heavy blanket was delivered as Reney was handed to her mother. Vera wrapped the child and held her tightly to her chest.

The men in the water still struggled with Daisy, urging her to let go of the rocks. She was unrecognizable to Laney. In place of her cap, a white mantle flowed from her head. It swept toward the creek, then rocked back, curling, and floated out again in the tow. As she was lifted up it fell heavily from her face, stretching down her back.

When Daisy had been hoisted over the fence, the car was leaving, carrying Vera with Reney, and two wet men.

Harv called to the driver, "Bring the car right back!"

"We can take Laney, now! Wanta come, Laney?"

"No, I'm staying!" she shouted. She had found a man's jacket, and now wrapped it around Daisy, trying to hold her tightly enough to stop her from shaking. The heavy, wet strands on her head and shoulders shone in the moonlight like slow-burning, silvery fire.

BRANCHING OUT

"So, you live right here in town, then?"

Laney Mahler, seventeen, glanced up at the man who had spoken to her over the counter at the soda fountain where she was working. The stranger looked older then herself; she guessed him to be in his early twenties.

Pumping chocolate syrup into a milkshake can, she took her time answering. She didn't like the man—didn't like his too-friendly manner, didn't like his shiny brown suit and loud tie, which were cheap-looking and too dressy for the small town, even on a Saturday night. And she didn't like the way he hunched forward on the counter as if trying to get closer.

"Yes, I live in town," she answered, turning aside to scoop vanilla ice cream.

"She lives in Plum Bottom," said Rita, Laney's co-worker, who was listening in.

"I know where that is," the man said, nodding. "Down by the Kingman River."

"Yeah," Rita went on, "down there where it floods every year." Grinning, she checked her flame-red fingernails.

Laney looked at her. "No, it doesn't. It floods maybe every few years. And usually it just covers a small area." She set the milkshake can onto the mixer.

While the mixer whirred, Rita sent the stranger a knowing smirk, as if to say, *Did you get that? She's sensitive about i*t.

"Besides," Laney added, "the town's planning a flood-abatement program, and soon there won't be any flooding at all." She removed the milkshake from the machine, poured most of it into a glass, and set both can and glass before the man. Then, taking his quarter off the counter, she said, "You don't live here, do you?"

"Nah, I'm just passing through," he said.

"Where do you live, then?" asked Rita.

"Over in Fenning, four miles up the road."

"Oh, yes, I like Fenning," Rita said. "It's nice over there."

The store had been crowded and noisy since the early movie had let out; the theater was just two buildings up the street. Now, at nearly ten o'clock, it was quieting down as people were leaving. Laney glanced back at the booths and saw that some needed clearing, while the sink was already stacked with dirty dishes. She headed for the sink area to start washing up.

As she ran fresh water, she saw the stranger moving down the counter to stand across from her again. His thin face was almost handsome, in a sharp-boned way, she thought, but his teeth looked uncared-for, and his hair was too thin for the small pompadour, à la Elvis.

He hunched his shoulders over the counter as he had done before. "You still in high school, or what?"

Laney looked toward the pharmacy, on her far right, behind a wide glass window. With surprise she saw Tom Josephs, the druggist, standing and staring straight at her. She met his eyes, then continued washing glasses. "I've just graduated from high school, and I'll start college in the fall."

"I thought you might. Where're you going to college?"

"We'd better start clearing the booths," she said to Rita, who had rejoined her after carrying cokes to a booth.

The man leaned conspiratorially closer. "I was thinking, I could give you a ride home after work, if you want."

Suddenly, Tom Josephs appeared beside the man. He tapped him on the shoulder, muttering a few low words.

The man straightened in surprise and cast Laney a quick look. Then Tom accompanied him past the gift and perfume counters, toward the door. The man tried to slouch and appear nonchalant, until Tom took his upper arm; then he hustled. At the door he stepped outside quickly, and disappeared into the night.

"Darn! Why'd Tom have to do that?" Rita said, standing beside Laney with a dishtowel. "He wasn't hurting anybody. He was kind of cute. Didn't you think he was kind of cute?"

"Rita! He was *just passing through*. Did you hear him say that? He came over here looking for a quick date. We don't know anything about him; we don't even know his name."

"So? He was certainly well dressed. You're suspicious of everyone. I'd've gone out with him in a minute." Sulkily she gave a wipe to a hot glass and set it on the shelf. "Of course, *you*. He was flirting with you, not me. You're the pretty one."

Laney spoke dully, without looking up from her dishes. "You're a pretty girl, Rita. You have nothing to feel bad about."

"My red hair is out of the bottle, you know."

"So? It looks good on you."

"Well, I do try. I have a better shape than you. My boobs are twice as big as yours."

"That's true."

"And you wear glasses sometimes, and I don't have to. That's a plus."

"Very true."

"But then, you've got Jon Boyer coming in here all the time. He heads straight for you, Laney. Everybody knows it."

"Right." She blew out a weary sigh. "He gets a coke, and we talk a little. That's not a date. Besides, he's working out of town."

"And you'd love to go out with him, right?"

Laney was about to say, "Sure, I would," but glanced at Rita and decided not to say it.

"It's okay, you can tell me. I'm good at keeping secrets."

"What I'd love to do is clean up and get out of here," said Laney. She dried her hands and handed Rita a tray.

Rita stood looking at it, then started out with it toward the booths.

———

Laney had fallen in love the previous year, when she was a junior in high school and Jon Boyer, a senior. Sharing no classes with Jon, she'd had little opportunity to even see him, mostly just as they passed in the halls. Her best opportunity was at band practice, though she played a clarinet and Jon a trumpet, which placed them at opposite sides of the band.

He had been a basketball star, and she had clipped photos of him from the school newspaper—always Jon with other team players. At night she had probed the pictures with her eyes, searching for the very heart of him, filling herself with the joy of a first love and the misery of finding it unattainable.

While not particularly handsome, Jon had an engaging grin and an easy, confident manner that made him very attractive to her. Occasionally, she came near him in the band locker room, where the members crowded together, laughing and talking as they collected or stowed their instruments. Once, as they were donning their uniforms in the school bathrooms, Laney had rushed back to the locker room for a clarinet reed and found Jon still there. He had been stooping to tie a shoe, and when she rushed in, he stood up. For an electrifying moment, their eyes met.

"Hi, Laney. How's it going?" he had said.

"I'm fine, thanks." *He spoke my name!*

She bobbed her head and hurried out before he could see the flush she felt rising in her face. In the hall, she cursed herself for being such an awkward dolt in his presence.

She had loved marching band—loved the complicated field maneuvers, loved seeing Jon marching along in his uniform with his sure, exact steps. Part of the pleasure had been traveling by bus to other schools. She had especially liked the ride home afterward, gliding along in the dark after the noisy bus had quieted enough that she could sometimes hear Jon's voice from the back, where he sat with the gang of athletes.

Late one night, after a long trip home, the band was rowdier than usual. Mr. Voris, the bandleader, wore himself out trying to quiet them and shout instructions for the following day. As the bus nosed into the school parking lot, band members were already out of their seats and crowding toward the exit, then piling out as soon as the door opened.

Laney was pushed along with the rest of the crowd toward the doorway's two downward steps. She maneuvered the first one, but then a sudden shove from behind caused her to go flying forward into a face-down sprawl on the asphalt. Next came a crushing blow when the girl behind her, who had also been pushed, tripped and landed on top of her.

In the ensuing scramble of uniformed legs, Laney felt the loudly weeping girl being lifted from her back. At last, Laney was raised to her knees by several hands. One of the faces in the crowd above her was Jon's.

Sitting up, she gathered her wits and decided that she hadn't been seriously hurt. As Mr. Voris bent down and questioned her, Laney found her voice to tell him she was alright.

Then Jon stooped, reached under her knees, and easily lifted her off the ground. Her father, who had been waiting in his car, came running over in alarm.

"I'm okay, Dad. I just fell out of the bus," she said, laughing shakily.

Jon carried her to the car, a slightly embarrassing trip for Laney, with her father walking beside them. "You can put me down, Jon," she said, and he carefully lowered her beside the passenger door.

As she straightened her legs, she had to mutter, "Ow". One knee hurt, and both hands. One palm had a scrape that was bleeding slightly. "Nothing serious," she said, although the hand burned like fire.

"Can I do anything more?" Jon asked.

"No," her dad said, glancing at Laney, "I think we'll be alright. Thanks for your help, son. What's your name?"

"Jon Boyer."

I forgot to introduce them! "This is my father, Jon. You probably guessed that."

"Yes. Hi, Mr. Mahler," he said, reaching to shake his hand. Then, wonder of wonders, he patted Laney's shoulder and let his hand linger there for a moment.

Driving home with her spirits soaring, Laney cradled her sore hands in her lap as she told her dad that the fall was not a big deal, nothing to get her mother upset about.

But to Laney, it was a very big deal. The memory of Jon's strong arms carrying her, and the lingering shoulder pat, would stay with her for years.

In the following weeks, Jon started coming into the drugstore while she was working. In Rita's words, he always headed straight for her.

"Here comes your lover again," Rita said, looking up from spooning cashews over hot fudge and pointing with her chin toward the tall, blond athlete striding into the store.

Laney broke into a delighted smile as Jon approached the counter.

"Hi, folks. Where's the girl who fell off the bus?"

Laney laughed as her hands reached automatically to the countertop, where he laid his warm hands over them. The touch, to Laney, was a pure thrill. "Hi, Jon!" she said. "I didn't know you were in town! How long will you be here?"

"I have to go back to work tonight. I was here yesterday, too. Mostly down at the gym, with a bunch of the guys."

"I'm glad you came in!" Then, remembering Tom in the pharmacy, she spoke more softly. "Want your usual Coke?"

"Yeah, with ice, please. You're a sight to behold, Laney." He gave her the crinkly-eyed smile that she loved. "Oh, man, it's good to be back home. Not that I don't like it where I work. Do you know where that is?"

"I've heard it's a hotel, somewhere around Fallsburg."

"Actually, it's a resort, just outside the town. The Vernal Springs Hotel. Ever hear the name? It's pretty famous."

"A resort! No, I've never heard of it. What kind of work do you do?"

"I'm a bellhop right now. But I'm thinking of staying on and trying to work my way up into management." He reached for his Coke and straw. "Which brings me to what I'm really here for. How would you like a summer job there as a waitress?"

She stared at him blankly. "A waitress at the resort?"

"Yep. You'd make good money, more than you make here, I'm sure. Waitresses get tips as well as their pay. And it's a beautiful place, Laney. It just so happens, they're hiring waitresses now. They need *fifty* waitresses for the summer. Imagine!"

"*Fifty*? The place must be huge! But where would I live? Would I have a room there?

"You'd stay in the waitress dormitory. Bellhops and busboys live in a sort of rundown part of the hotel. Waitresses have it better—they have a big, old ramshackle building to themselves."

"Really?" But she had to pause and think. "I don't know, Jon. I've only been away from home a few times, mostly just at my grandparents'."

"Time to branch out, Laney. You'll have to leave home for college."

"True. But then, there's my parents. They may not allow it."

"Why not? You'd be absolutely safe. They watch that dorm like a hawk. And think of the friends you'd make. All college-age kids, or just out of high school. We have fun there, Laney. We get time off. Sometimes a bunch of us pile into a taxi and ride into town. Taxis are dirt cheap, going with a group."

"It does sound like fun."

"I don't have a car yet, but I soon will. Right now a guy there lets me borrow his. Maybe you could ride home with me sometimes."

"Could I? I'd love that! Okay, I'll talk it over with my folks."

Jon gave her his phone number at work, saying he would need her decision by the following evening. If she said yes, he would get her an appointment for a job interview, and call her with the details. "Unfortunately," he added, "the interviews are always on Mondays, and I know your dad works all week."

"That's true, but this is important!" The thought of traveling in a car with Jon had made the idea too tempting to refuse. "For this, I think Dad would be willing to take a day off."

It was easier than Laney had anticipated to convince her parents that she should take the job at the hotel. She would be safe, making new friends, and earning more money than she would at the drugstore. "The tips are really good, Jon says, and I'd get some regular pay, besides."

Her five-year-old sister, Reney, was the only one displeased. "Why don't you stay here? You've got a good job *here*."

"Don't worry," Laney said, smoothing back the child's wispy braids. "It's just for the summer. Even when I'm in college, I'll keep coming home."

"Jon will be there," her dad said. "It won't be as if she doesn't know anyone."

In a state of pure delight, Laney telephoned Jon, who promised to call her back when he had scheduled her interview.

Then came a surprise. He didn't call.

Day after day passed, as she continued working in the drugstore. June arrived, and she became increasingly worried. "I don't even know if they're still hiring," she told her dad. "We're into the summer tourist season, now."

"Probably some girls quit from time to time," Harv said. "They'd have to be replaced, wouldn't they?"

Finally came the call. Jon sounded subdued, perhaps tired, Laney thought. But he had kept his word. She had an appointment with the maître d' the following Monday morning.

———∞∞∞———

It was raining Monday as Laney and her father climbed into their car and set out for the Vernal Springs Hotel. Not knowing how to dress for the occasion, she had first chosen a silky, Sunday dress with nylons and heels. Then, deciding it was better to be underdressed than overdressed, she ended up wearing a well-ironed cotton skirt and blouse with flat shoes.

Harv seemed unusually quiet, as they started the hour-long trip. He had insisted on wearing his suit, in case he would have to walk her into the building. The hotel, of which her parents knew very little, loomed awesomely in Laney's mind. And her father's solemn face suggested to her that he might be even more apprehensive than she was.

"You know, Laney, you might not get this job," he said. "I don't think you should count on it too strong. You might not be experienced enough. I don't even know if working in a drugstore is the right kind of experience."

"I know that, Dad. Don't worry, I won't be too disappointed if I fail. But I want to give it a try. You know, starting college this fall may not be easy. Freshmen aren't allowed to see their folks the whole first six weeks. This job should help me get used to being away from home. Jon says it's time for me to branch out."

"Well, he's right about that. And I don't think he'd have given you a bum steer."

The rain had tapered off as they drove into the hotel's huge parking lot, where a scattering of cars were separated by rows of trees. Through the slight drizzle, a large cream-and-white building appeared: a structure made long by extensions—one end turning in at a slight angle, and the other end, which looked like a glassed-in porch, projecting forward. Driving nearer through leafy trees, they saw white-shuttered windows and an upper story with balcony railings. Four tall, white columns framed the front entrance, and, in the center, a porte-cochère extended outward over the driveway. Laney saw that she'd be able to get inside without getting wet.

Harv, who had intended to park with the other cars, instead followed Laney's urging to pull under the porte-cochère. "I don't think I should stay here, Laney," he said. "I'm going to park in the lot, near the front. You don't need me to walk you in, do you?"

"No, just wait in the car. I'm on time, and it shouldn't take too long."

He nodded and wished her good luck.

Leaving the roofed area, Laney climbed two wide steps and reached a heavy glass door, which was opened for her by a man in uniform. *Doorman,* she thought, returning his smile. He wished her a good morning, and she thanked him.

Straight ahead was the reception area. On soft, red-print carpet, she proceeded to the counter, where a woman and a man were working quietly. To the right, a gleaming dark-wood staircase curved upward, leading, she presumed, to luxurious bedrooms upstairs.

The woman and man both looked up at Laney's approach. The woman, with a model's perfectly made-up face, smiled sweetly at Laney. But then the smile disappeared, and Laney sensed that something was wrong.

"May I help you, Miss?" the woman asked.

"Yes, please. I'm here for an interview for a waitress job. With Mister Joyce."

"A waitress job? My dear, you don't come in through the front door. Waitresses *never* come in the front entrance." She spoke gently, but seriously.

"Oh, I'm sorry! I didn't know. Where...? I...," Laney stammered.

"Go back outside and down the steps, turn right, and walk clear around the end of the building, till you reach the back street. You'll have to walk through the grass."

"The grass is wet, Emma," the man discreetly interjected.

"Well...." She hesitated.

"I think we can let her go through the dining room," the man continued. "Mister Joyce has a little waiting room outside his office. It's near the back entrance."

The woman pursed her lips. "Then, I guess she'll have to go on through. Don't speak to anyone in there, though," she cautioned. "Especially not to guests."

Somewhat shaken, Laney murmured a thank you as she walked past the counter. Ahead were French doors, through which she saw many white-clothed tables. As she stepped through the doorway, a tall man wearing what appeared a black tuxedo was hurrying to intercept her.

"Are you a guest, Miss?" he said, frowning as he reached her.

"No." *Not again!* "I'm here for an interview with Mister Joyce."

"I see. But you can't come in this way."

"I'm sorry. I made a mistake. But the lady out front said...."

"I don't care what she said. Waitresses enter the dining room *only* through the kitchen. You had no business even passing through the front of the hotel."

Laney looked about her, nonplussed. "I think I'd have to walk a long way, in the grass, and it's wet. It's still raining. And I don't have an umbrella."

"That is regrettable," he said stiffly, "isn't it?"

"Oh, for Christ's sake, let her come in!" growled a deep voice from a nearby table, where a man looked up from his lunch.

The tall man fell silent. Then he said tersely, "Go down this aisle. Then turn right, and go through the swinging doors. The *left* door. Don't go through the right door. In the kitchen, you'll ask for Mister Joyce."

Laney thanked him shakily and started down the aisle as directed. From behind her, she heard the uniformed man apologize to the diner, who replied in a lower voice, "It's the girl you ought to apologize to."

As Laney hurried past more tables and guests, she thought, *Not even hired yet*, *and already I've made myself an enemy.*

As she drew near the swinging doors, she slowed. Was she to go in the *left* door? That seemed awkward. Why not the right door, which would be her natural choice? She stood confused until suddenly the right door burst open and a waitress came flying through it, carrying over her shoulder, on raised fingertips, a heavily-loaded tray.

Laney stepped out of the way and proceeded through the left door, grateful to have the situation explained for her and wondering how the girl could possibly balance such a heavy tray on her fingertips.

———

Mr. Joyce introduced himself to her as "Danny". Not much taller than Laney, nearly bald, he looked Irish to her, with brilliant blue eyes and a wide straight mouth that fleetingly reminded her of a frog. With a downward-looking, head-ducking walk, he escorted her through a huge barn of a kitchen to his office.

"Come in, come in," he said, taking her shoulder and drawing her brusquely into a small, cluttered room. He placed a chair for her so closely facing his own, Laney was concerned that their knees would touch.

When she sat, she inched her chair slightly backward, while Danny squeezed past her into his chair. Both seated, they faced each other. Leaning closer, he looked deeply into her eyes. She sat up straight, confused by such intimacy.

Then he ducked to one side, taking a clipboard from a shelf and glancing at it.

"Laney, that's a pretty name." He inched forward again and resumed studying her face. "And you're a very pretty girl, Laney. Nice, too. You *are* a nice girl, aren't you? Of course, you are. And you're how old?" He glanced again toward his clipboard.

"I'll be eighteen this summer," Laney said, to be helpful. "I'll be starting college this fall."

"Very good. Excellent." He nodded abruptly. Then, leaning even closer, he laid a large hand on her leg, just above the knee.

Laney started, her mind in a whirl. *Oh, no! I have to say something, and then I'll lose the job!* But her hands were moving on their own accord, gently lifting his hand off her leg.

The hand would have dropped, but he swung it smoothly back to the shelf, and, chuckling lightly, he dug under the clipboard for a sheet of paper.

Sitting back again, he looked at the paper. "Now, then, what's your experience, Laney? Do you *have* any work experience?"

"I've worked part-time in a drugstore for a year and a half. Mostly at the soda fountain."

"What do you mean, part-time?"

"Actually, it was full-time last summer. During the winter I had school, of course, and just worked three nights a week."

"And what did you do the other nights?"

Why should he want to know this? "I played the organ for choir practice one night, and men's chorus practice another night. And I played for Sunday night church."

"My goodness! You've lived a churchy life, haven't you?"

She paused, then murmured, "I guess so."

"And, how about at work. You carried food to tables?"

"Yes.... Well, booths."

"Mm-*hmm*. That's good. It's not good, but it's alright. You don't really need experience here. We train our beginners. We want them to do things *our* way." He dropped his chin and looked at her from under his brows. "Kapeesh?"

She made an uncertain nod.

"So...you'll need to be here Saturday morning, early. You'll meet with Ronnie, our hostess. She works with the waitresses—gets them uniforms, teaches them to carry trays, everything. You'll find her in the waitress dormitory, outside this open door."

He gestured back toward a wide doorway, where Laney had seen uniformed girls come and go. "There's an alley back there, behind the hotel. It comes straight in from the main road. You can't park your car there, but you can stop to unload your suitcases." He briefly explained the salary plan: she would receive a small hourly wage in addition to her tips.

"So, that's it? I'm hired?"

"Of course! Of course!" He arose then, scooting his chair back. Before she could stand up, he patted her on the head.

Then he smiled widely, gestured toward the door with a flourish, and let her precede him out of the room.

There she spoke. "Mr. Joyce, my dad's car is parked out front. I need to go out the front way. But I was stopped when I tried to come in through the dining room. The man in the black uniform…."

Danny made a comical, scowling face. "That's Jack, the head waiter. He's full of himself. You tell him Danny said to *lay off*."

"But if he—"

"You tell him Danny is the boss. Danny is *his* boss."

"So it'll be alright?" she asked, still skeptical.

"Of course, of course!" Reaching around her from the side, he gave her hip a friendly pat.

As she left, she came close to laughing, remembering his roaming hands. *What a weirdo, but he's kind of nice. And I'm hired! Hallelujah!*

In the big, open kitchen, waitresses were moving back and forth, mostly sliding trays on gleaming steel ledges to pick up dishes. Laney paused to watch a nearby waitress. One by one, the girl lifted four loaded plates, each topped with a large aluminum lid, and stacked them two by two on her tray. Then she expertly swung the tray up to her shoulder. Turning to face Laney, she jerked her free thumb toward Danny's office and rolled her eyes, grinning.

Laney nodded, laughing quietly.

"You comin' in when, tomorrow?" the girl asked.

"No, Thursday. He gave me two days to pack and get ready."

"I'll *see* ya! You and me might be partners in the dining room! My name's Patch." She looked Laney's age or younger, with a slightly crooked jaw and a mischievous grin. "Wanna be partners with me?"

"Yes!" Laney said. "I'm Laney."

Then Danny came hustling by with a mock sour look. "Don't believe a thing Patch says."

Patch's eyes twinkled as she raised the tray to her fingertips. Then she hurried away with it poised beside her ear, and the other arm stuck out slightly for balance. Laney happily followed her through the left swinging door and into the dining room.

Ahead lay the gauntlet she had passed on her way in.

What luck! At the French doors, "Jack" was nowhere in sight. Then she breezed past the reception desk, sending a smile to the woman who had reluctantly helped her, and who now gave her a tiny wave.

When she reached the car, her father asked if she had been hired. She answered with an exultant grin, "Of course! Of course!"

⸺⸙⸺

Laney had been scheduled to work at the drugstore on Friday, the very day before her waitress job started at the resort. Knowing that Tom Josephs needed her at work, she kept to the schedule, though she would rather have had the day at home. As she left for work Friday morning, her mother gave her an unexpected hug and, with unusual gravity, told her daughter she would miss her terribly in the days ahead.

But, as Laney returned the hug, her thoughts were in such a joyful blur that they skipped lightly over her mother's concern. She had happy plans. It would be fun working today, saying good-bye to everyone—even to friends who came in the door. She had bought Reney a new book, which they would read together tonight. Then she would take her time packing, carefully folding her freshly washed and ironed clothes.

In the drugstore, Tom came out of the pharmacy to wish her happiness in her new job, and warmly shook her hand in both of his. Then Laney and Rita tackled their regular Friday morning job of cleaning the fountain area. Rita had become so quiet that Laney, sensing the girl's disappointment with her now dull-seeming life, quelled her own exuberance. But the joy that needed expressing kept her smiling happily to customers and anyone passing by.

In mid-afternoon, she was washing dishes when she suddenly looked up. She thought she had heard Jon's voice. With her heart quickening, she reached for a towel to dry her hands. Jon was home? He hadn't been in the drugstore for such a long time.

As he came strolling in, his eyes searched the fountain area, and finding her, he grinned. He looked freshly scrubbed, with his face and arms a rosy tan. He called ahead to her, "Taken any bus trips lately?"

"Hi there!" She laughed, delighted. "No, one trip was enough. It looks like you've been out in the sun."

"True, I have. I play a little golf, lately. You're looking wonderful, as usual." As he spoke, he turned toward an attractive girl who was stepping up to stand beside him.

The girl spoke a shy "Hello." Dark hair cut fashionably short; tan arms in a white, sleeveless dress.

Laney answered with an uncertain-sounding "Hello."

Jon slipped an arm around the girl's shoulders and drew her closer as he spoke. "Laney, I'd like you to meet Sheila Berman. She works with me at the Springs. She's my girl-friend. Matter of fact—she's agreed to become my fiancée." He smiled proudly, his eyes on Sheila. Then, indicating Laney, he said, "This is the pretty girl I told you about."

Laney stood as if frozen.

Then, almost immediately, she became two persons: one who was so shocked that she thought she might faint, and the other who nodded politely and said she was happy to meet the girl.

Sheila said in a self-deprecating way, "It's going to have to be a long engagement."

"We both need to work and save money," Jon explained. "Sheila works year-round at the Springs. They keep a small staff there in the winter, and I'm hoping to get hired year-round, too, so we can be together." His hand moved up and down on her bare arm.

Then they ordered Cokes, which Laney served with a stiff smile. As more customers approached the counter, she turned away numbly to wait on a new party. Then another, and another, grateful to be busy while Jon and Sheila huddled over their Cokes.

Finally, they turned to go. As they left, Jon called back cheerily, "I'll be seeing you at the hotel, Laney."

Rita, who had stayed clear of Laney's predicament, now came to stand beside her.

"Oh, my *Lord*, Laney!" she said under her breath. "Are you okay? Oh, my God, I'm so sorry!" Rita peered into Laney's eyes, which were filling with tears, then reached an arm around her waist, and leaned her head sideways to touch Laney's.

"Thanks, Rita. You're a good friend." Laney sniffed and reached for a napkin. "I've never put on such an act before in my whole life." Turning her back to the counter, she blew her nose quietly, using the napkin. "I guess I know where I stand now."

"What a jerk!" Rita said. "Who'd'a thought? But men are like that, Laney. Honest to God, they are. I don't really trust the guys I date, either. 'Cause men are fickle, and they're liars. *All* of them."

"Rita, just tell me one thing, would you?"

"Sure. Name it."

"How obvious have I been all this time? I mean, acting like I was his girl?"

"Pretty darn obvious. How could you help it? He *called* you his girl. I've heard him say it, more than once. And coming in to see you all the time…."

"Okay. So I made a fool of myself."

"Not really. You never went that far. I mean, you didn't crow about it or anything." She watched Laney dry her eyes. "You can tell people you broke up. No…, wait a minute…, you don't want that."

"No. Anyway, it's not true. He dumped me." Laney picked up the stack of napkins and made an awkward attempt at straightening them. "I'll just have to live it down, as they say."

Rita had another thought. "Oh, my God, you poor girl! You have to go over there and work with him…, and with her, too! Oh, sweet Jesus!"

"I know. It's terrible. I can't stand the thought of going to that place, now."

"Well, maybe you can get out of it."

"How?" Laney asked. "I made a commitment! They expect me, tomorrow morning!"

"Couldn't you just phone the hotel and tell them you can't come? Tell them something came up. You have to go away for the summer. Some family member got sick and you have to go stay with them."

"I couldn't lie like that, Rita."

"Well, you're too damn honest. How many waitresses do they have?"

"A lot. Fifty."

"*Fifty* waitresses? And you think they'd miss *one*?" Rita was getting loud.

"Shhh!" Laney looked warily toward the pharmacy. "At least, I haven't packed. My clothes are all clean and ready, but not packed, yet. My poor parents. They'll be so shocked. I'll have to see what they think about me possibly not going."

"To heck with them, Laney, it's your decision! You're the one who'd have to go over there and face him. And her."

Just then, a noisy softball team started coming in the door, and the girls became busy. Laney worked with an eye on the clock, anxious to get home and, at the same time, dreading it.

Her mother's mouth fell open as Laney told her what had transpired in the drugstore. "Oh, my *Lord*, Laney," she swore, astonished. "You don't mean it."

"Just like that, Mom. He dumped me, plain and simple." Then she stopped short because her voice was breaking.

Her father appeared in the doorway carrying his opened newspaper. "What's this?"

"Laney says Jon just told her he's engaged to some other girl!"

"I'm not sure I ever *was* his girl," Laney said tearfully. "We never had a date.... There was practically nothing between us. I can see that now. I was just...I'm all screwed up. I can't think anymore."

Reney, who had just run into the kitchen, looked up at her. "Don't cry, Laney."

"And he's engaged to the girl." Harv had finally found his voice. "That means he's been going with her for some time."

"While he was coming into the drugstore to see you!" said her mother. "Just stringing you along."

"I was so fooled by that," said Laney. "How could I have been such an idiot?"

"You're not the only one who was fooled," Harv commiserated. "I was completely taken in. I *liked* the boy."

"I *hate* him," said Reney.

"No, he's not a bad person," Laney said dully. "I think he just found this girl over there and couldn't bring himself to tell me about her. Maybe he was too embarrassed."

"The word *cowardly* comes to mind," Harv said.

"Well, what are you going to do now?" her mother asked, opening the hot oven door. and peering in. "What about your job, working in the hotel with him? Do you still want to go through with it?"

Laney looked up, heartened. They weren't going to press her to go. "I'm thinking about it, Mom. I'm not packed yet. I know Tom would be glad to keep me on at the drugstore. And Linda isn't quite ready to take over the organ at church. We just have to decide tonight."

"Well," Harv said, "I think it's your decision. It would probably be easier all around if you stayed home, and kept on at the drugstore. You'll be leaving for college anyway, soon enough."

"Oh, good, you're not going, then!" said Reney. "Ya-ay!"

"You'd better phone the hotel tonight," Vera said. "They'll be serving dinner over there. Harv, you could call up Long Distance and get their phone number."

"I think it can wait till tomorrow, Vera. I'll get the number tonight, but I think she could call them in the morning." Laney watched a clouded look cross his face. "It's a shame, in a way. She was so happy after that interview, coming out to tell me she had the job."

Vera's voice sharpened slightly. "You think she'd be that happy working there every day, trying to avoid the boy?"

"No," he said calmly. "Everything's changed, now, I can see that."

Laney began to relax. The situation was so much easier than she'd expected that relief was pouring over her. She didn't even have to pack. She'd make the phone call in the morning, and tonight she could actually rest. Humbled, she sat down to dinner with her family, aware of their protective love around her like a blanket.

After helping with the dishes, she read storybooks with Reney, pausing often for the child to supply the next word. Sometimes this practice put them both to sleep, but not tonight. Still wakeful after tucking the girl into bed, Laney went back downstairs as her parents were preparing to go up.

In the living room, she turned the television on low and settled herself comfortably on the couch. *The Hit Parade* was on, but after the first couple songs her thoughts drifted and she became oblivious to the figures on the small screen. Doubts she had suppressed were beginning to re-emerge.

When I call the hotel, what if they connect me with Danny himself? Can I tell him a good, convincing lie? Will he yell at me, or possibly even shame me into coming to work, after all?

And, if I did go tomorrow and started work, would I be able to stay clear of Jon? How often are waitresses and bellhops thrown together? Would I have to keep seeing him all summer? She hugged her arms, imagining her shame and embarrassment.

But if I kept on working in the drugstore, what could I tell people there? What would I tell Jenny? And wouldn't the summer here be long and boring? Wouldn't I regret giving up an exciting new job? And the extra money—how much could I have earned in tips?

She arose, turned off the television, which was showing its "off the air" pattern, and started up the stairs in the dark.

Then, awake in bed, she finally faced the worst pain of all. She'd known it was there, underlying all her other concerns, waiting to rise when her defenses were down. Staring into the dark ceiling, she acknowledged to herself that Jon did not love her, and probably never had. Tears sprang instantly.

Did he even know that I loved him? He must have known! I practically climbed over the counter to reach him when he came into the store.

It was so humiliating! Who knew humiliation could hurt so much? She didn't like to think of herself as proud, but maybe she had this coming. Pride goeth..., she thought grimly.

Keeping it quiet, she let herself cry into her pillow for what seemed like hours, until finally she reached a state of something like acceptance.

At last, she was able to weigh everything about her situation. She started to think more clearly.

Toward morning, she got up, turned on a soft light, and started to pack.

———

"Laney! What are you up so early for?" her mother said, hurrying into the living room in her robe. "You could have slept in!" Then she saw Laney's two small suitcases by the door and stopped short, staring at them. "Oh, for heaven's sake!"

"Hi, Mom. Strange things happened in the night." She laughed quietly.

"For *heaven's* sake!" Vera said again.

"I just couldn't be so chicken as to skip out on this job, Mom. I got thrown off track there for a while, but I've gotten over it. I still want the job. I'm not going to let Jon ruin it for me."

"You've got dark hollows under your eyes, Laney."

"Actually, I feel pretty good. I'm drinking coffee, and it's pepping me up."

"What's this?" Harv walked in with his graying hair askew. "You want to go over there today, after all?"

"Yes. I hope you can still take me," Laney replied.

"Sure, I can! With pleasure! I'd planned to take the day off, anyway." Harv smoothed back his hair with both hands, chuckling.

"Well, who'd have thought!" her mother exclaimed. "Are you positively sure about this, Laney?"

"Yep, I'm sure. I liked the place when I was there. And I liked the girl I told you about. She said we might be partners. And just think, a dormitory! That sounds like fun to me. I'll get to see it today, and move in!"

"But *why* did you change your mind?" Reney wailed, joining them in her pajamas and trailing a stuffed rabbit. "You said you were staying home!"

Laney sat down and took the girl's arms in her hands. "I need to go, honey. I'll be earning more money for college. And I need to try new things, and find new friends. You'll be doing that yourself, when you start school in the fall."

"We could drive over there and visit Laney sometime, Vera," Harv said. "What do you think?"

"What *I'd* like to do," Vera said, setting out cereal bowls, "is to come through the front door of that place and be treated like a guest."

"You'll be treated like royalty!" Laney said. "And if you have lunch there, I'll make sure I wait on you, myself. Or, me and Patch will, as she would say. I hope we don't drop a tray, or spill anything on you."

The glum Reney climbed into her chair and reached for her milk, muttering, "Just so it isn't something hot."

LEAVING PLUM BOTTOM

As the road curved southward around the Vernal Springs Resort Hotel, it first passed emerald green lawns with rhododendrons glowing pink and red at the peak of their season, and beyond them, a velvety green golf course that meandered over sculpted knolls. Next came the sprawling hotel itself, emerging through trees, with shuttered windows and a high-columned front entrance. Just past the hotel, a large swimming pool lay sparkling in the sun, its painted sides turning the water a bright cerulean blue.

A little further south, a side road branched westward off the main highway, then turned sharply toward the back side of the hotel, where it narrowed to an alley stretching past the waitress dormitory. There it entered a different world.

The dormitory was a white, two-story building, paint-peeled and weather-beaten. Beyond it, the alley widened into a broader space to accommodate trucks that brought food into the hotel and trucks that hauled garbage out. In this area were a small, dingy-looking cafeteria and the back entrance to the hotel kitchen. Here a row of bins gave out an aroma, redolent of rotting vegetables, which blended with the cafeteria's indefinably foody smell and lingered in the air, usually mild but strengthening in hot weather.

For all this world's unsavory odors and rundown appearance, an aura persisted of something pleasant: a hint of the resort's glamour, which was confined to the front of the hotel, leaking through somehow to the waitress dormitory; a sense of it being vacation time, even though the vacation was for guests; always a mild excitement in the air, rich with possibility for young girls who worked hard in the dining room and, on their free hours, dreamed of romance.

Singing could sometimes be heard, drifting down from the dorm's upstairs windows, while uniformed girls walked to and from the hotel kitchen, laughing and talking, jingling change in their apron pockets. Today, radio music poured down into the alley—Johnny Ray, sobbing, "If your sa-*weet* heart...sends a let-*ter*...of good-*bye*—". It was mid-June, 1952.

On the dormitory's small porch, the door stood open wide, revealing a narrow staircase that led upwards. At the top, an open floor space held several ironing boards standing askew, with irons and dangling cords.

Near the ironing boards stood Ronnie Shoals, the dining room hostess, in her black skirt and ruffled white blouse, and Laney Mahler, wearing a sleeveless cotton dress that reached below her knees. Ronnie, holding an ashtray, was making soft, puffing sounds with a cigarette. Laney had been traveling up and down the dorm's long hallway, tray-practicing with a suitcase. Now she rested, and thought her own thoughts.

The knowledge that Jon Boyer and his fiancée were nearby lay just below the surface in Laney's mind, occasionally rising like a twinge of pain. On this, her first day, the dorm and hotel kitchen seemed safely removed from a bellhop's more elegant world. But as for the dining room itself—she'd have to wait and see.

Ronnie sucked once more on her cigarette, then crushed it in her ashtray. "Come on," she said, "let's get at it again. We still need to pick up your uniforms, and I have things of my own to do."

Laney positioned herself as Ronnie had instructed her. With her right hand raised by her shoulder, she arranged her upward-pointing fingers with thumb and little finger stretched forward and the other three back. The medium-sized, rounded suitcase that Ronnie placed on her fingertips felt as light as cardboard; Laney thought it would have been easier to balance if it had a little weight.

"Keep your hand *back!* I told you, Laney, behind your ear! Keep your face to the side!" Ronnie was trying to be patient and failing, jerking the suitcase back until Laney's shoulder creaked. "It won't fall—swing your elbow a little. Stick out your left arm for balance. Alright, now, take off down the hall and let it rock."

Laney took off, the suitcase teetering so far to the side that she could hardly see it. She had told Ronnie she was left-handed, but this had just annoyed her; left-handers made nothing but trouble in the kitchen, she'd said, so Laney had become an instant right-handed waitress.

"Don't look at it! Don't you dare become one of those scared ninnies that have to keep watching their tray!" Ronnie called, hurrying after her. "Now pretend you have three entrées swinging up there."

Laney trotted down the hall, with its worn floorboards and faded carpet runner. Reaching the end, with Ronnie following at a distance, she swung around—a wobbly turn, requiring both hands. Then up the hall again, passing Ronnie, who had stepped aside to give her room. A smoother turn at this end, and once again into the long stretch.

Something about it was starting to feel more right.

I knew I could learn how to do this.

There was an ease about it, after all, the weight on her fingers somehow transferring down the rest of her body. She straightened her head, and the suitcase rocked gently and surely, so much a part of her that nothing on it would have slid, not a plate or a bowl—hopefully, not even glasses of iced tea.

"That's better! You're getting it!" Ronnie called, running after her with her stocking legs scraping. "Keep going to the front end, then bring it down. Swing it forward and give it a twirl."

The twirl was easy. Spinning the suitcase forward, she gave it an assist from her left hand.

Too fast! Helplessly, Laney watched it slip and go flying off her fingertips to slam into one of the ironing boards, knocking it over and sending its iron crashing to the floor. Stumbling over ironing board legs, she scrambled after the suitcase.

Behind her, Ronnie planted her feet apart, stretching her tight skirt. "There, my sweet little babe, went *three expensive entrées!*"

In her early thirties, Laney guessed, she was pretty, except for a slight drooping of her face around the mouth. Atop her head, black hair gleamed in an arrangement of curls, beneath which her mascaraed eyes stared darkly.

Ronnie now made no attempt to conceal her anger as she righted the ironing board and slammed the iron back onto it. Laney, crestfallen, kept apologizing.

As they spoke, girlish voices rose from outside. The lunch shift was ending, with the first few waitresses returning to the dorm. Footsteps came pounding up the stairs, and two girls appeared, breathless and laughing, pulling off hairnets and shaking out their hair.

"Girls," Ronnie shouted to be heard, "this is Laney Mahler. She'll be starting on the floor tomorrow. Did you hear me? Slow down! This is Bettylu Weimer, Laney, and Barbara Miller."

"Hi, Laney, how're ya doing?"

"See you around!"

Laney said hello, happily sizing them up as friends-to-be.

Three more girls arrived; three more quick introductions. Then began a steady parade of waitresses, all wearing white shoes, seamless stockings, and pale yellow uniforms. Ronnie shortened her introductions to first names only, but they still became a blur in Laney's mind.

Finally, two late-comers arrived, moving more slowly. Ramona, plump and baby-faced, plodded up the stairs, unbuttoning her front as she climbed. Giving Laney a blank nod, she pulled her uniform off completely before turning down the hall, with breasts like melons swinging in her bra and a fat midriff bulging above her half-slip.

Laney looked to Ronnie, whose mouth was set in disgust.

Following Ramona, a taller girl named Kate paused to meet Laney. Apparently in her twenties, she had short red hair that stood up like a soft crew cut. She glanced at Laney's suitcase, and then at Ronnie. "I see you've got this skinny little kid under your wing." Her voice was slightly husky. "Teaching her with great patience, I'm sure."

"Mind your own business, snot! Move along! And tell your unconscious friend to quit undressing on the stairs! How'd she like it if some of the men walked by, and looked up here and saw her?"

"I don't know, I'll ask her. Hey, Ramona!"

"You sassy brat! You better be on the floor early tonight, if you know what's good for you! And get some white on those filthy shoes!" Angrily Ronnie spat a bit of cigarette paper off the tip of her tongue. "Unless you want to be bumped back out to the porch."

Kate lifted her freckled nose to say, "Bump away. I get good tips out there." From the side, she gave Laney a slow, green-eyed wink.

Laney stared after her as she sauntered down the hall.

"I wish to hell I could fire that girl," Ronnie muttered. "I would, if I didn't need her on the floor. Never mind her, Laney. She's a good one for you to avoid. You want to be careful," she added with a dark look, "who you choose for friends here."

The dining room seated three hundred, divided among the large main room, the north wing, and the window-walled porch. The atmosphere spoke of comfortable old wealth: the slightly path-worn carpet of a soft green, with a brighter green in the upholstered chairs; touches of gold-painted scrollwork on the walls, matching the gilt frames on large, dull, landscape paintings.

At the front entrance, two pedestals held large arrangements of fresh flowers. Mornings, while sunlight poured through the east windows, they were typically warm-colored—yellows, oranges, pinks. For dinner, with light from crystal chandeliers, new flowers appeared, in rich reds and purples, to go with the scarlet dinner menus. For evening, the waitress uniforms were also changed, from the daytime pale yellow to white.

While Laney felt awed by such grandeur, sarcastic Kate pointed out that the employees had their own color scheme: the waitresses all white, and the busboys all black.

Ronnie rewarded Laney for her tray-foibles by assigning her to work with Hilda, an experienced waitress in her fifties. Greatly disappointed, Laney begged to work with Patch, whom she had met the day she'd come for her job interview. But Ronnie told her a firm "No", saying that, with Hilda, she'd be learning from the best.

"And what am *I*, the worst?" asked the disgruntled Patch, as the two girls renewed their acquaintance standing outside the dormitory.

Laney had learned, with surprise, that Patch was here for her third summer. She had her own small station, two four-seater tables and a two-seater, or deuce, while waiting to be assigned a partner.

Laney first learned the order of service, while Hilda "ran the trays". Soon, Laney was running the lighter trays herself. Between the dining room and the kitchen were swinging doors, where the traffic seemed opposite from the pattern familiar to Laney: the into-kitchen door on the left and the out-from-kitchen door on the right. Behind the right door stood the checker's stand, where orders were checked before being brought out to the dining room; there, also, were ice and water, which always came out with the food. Hence, the entrance to the kitchen being on the left.

The swinging doors separated a world of quiet elegance from the sometimes crashing, yelling inferno of the kitchen. When the dining room was full, the atmosphere there became galvanized with tension, waitresses hurrying with trays, flipping anxiously through their checks, and chafing with impatience as they waited in line at the range.

Laney, passing carefully in and out of the kitchen, became leery of the busboys, who had a habit of running up behind an unsuspecting waitress, trampling on her heels, and muttering, "Hup, Hup!" until she got out of the way. Ronnie had warned her early not to cross the busboys, as they all stuck together, the black devils, and could make a waitress's life a pure hell if they wanted to.

On Laney's third night, Hilda developed an upset stomach, leaving Laney to work dinner alone. Ronnie gave her a small station, only one round six-seater, near Patch's tables.

"It's a perfect experience for you," Ronnie said, "one big party, and you can give them your full attention. Be *damn* careful. They're bigwigs…, three men from hotel management, entertaining guests. Don't forget finger bowls with chicken and frog legs. If you take any orders for *en casserole*, call me to serve them for you. I don't want you slopping food on the tablecloth in front of these men. Okay? Got all that?"

Laney nodded, quaking with apprehension.

Ronnie gave her a dubious glare and strode off, white earrings bouncing above her neck ruffles.

By the time Ronnie seated her six men, Laney had polished the flatware until it shone.

"Are you English?" one man asked her as she took their order. Her speech, ordinarily somewhat clipped and precise, had become more so with nervousness.

Of course. This is an English-speaking country, isn't it? She answered, "Yes."

"Aha!" he said happily to the other men. "I knew it! My mother was Australian."

Horrified at her mistake, from then on Laney spoke as little as possible. The men, apparently pleased with her shyness, tried to draw her out, while she gave short answers, sounding more British than ever. *Any second, one of them will ask me what part of England I'm from.*

As she carried the first two soups over from the tray stand, Ronnie suddenly appeared, hissing, "Salads!"

Laney had forgotten to remove their empty salad plates! She stood frozen, sloshing the soups into their underliners, as Ronnie slipped all six salads off the table without clattering a plate.

"Where are your biscuits?" came the next furious whisper.

Laney had forgotten to bring them in with the soups.

"Go get them! Serve those soups first, you idiot!" Ronnie served the other four as Laney got rid of her two. Then she lunged toward the kitchen, having to turn back for her tray—even for just biscuits, the tray was required.

Aflutter as she neared the doors, she approached the left with her hand out to push through it, then immediately thought she had forgotten the backwards rule.

This is the wrong door!

Jumping as if the floor mat were hot, she got away from the left door and in front of the right one—just as it burst open in her face. Out came a white jacket, and looming over her, a tray stacked with entrées.

Crash! A twining of arms and trays. Then she passed under the busboy's arm and ran into the doorframe. Behind her the nightmare went on, with clanging entrée covers and smashing china. As she looked back, the busboy was on his hands and knees in a mess of food and broken dishes. Silence had settled over the entire dining room.

Laney dropped to her knees beside him. She started picking up broken pieces of plate and reached for an entrée cover that had rolled away.

"What the hell you doin'?" the busboy asked furiously. He had gravy down his white front and reddish sauce in his black hair. "Git! You ain't supposed to help!"

She knew him remotely: Marlin, chief of the busboys.

"Jesus!" swore Jack, the tuxedoed headwaiter, standing over them looking stunned. Then he came to, snapping his fingers toward a busboy headed in their direction with an empty tray. "Get up, Mahler! On your feet! Not you, Marlin! *You! Girl!* Get out of here!"

Laney rose and stumbled through the left door into the kitchen. A little later, she was dashing past the checker's booth with a basket of biscuits on a new tray.

"What do you think you're doing?" the checker called. "Biscuits are served with soup!"

"I know, I forgot them," Laney called, and kept going. She made it nearly to the doors, when suddenly she was stopped— a black hand had grabbed her free arm, causing her biscuits to go flying. It was Marlin, reaching from inside the tiny room that was called the linen bin.

She stood helplessly in his grip while he glanced toward the checker, who was busy, and with one shiny black shoe, he kicked the biscuits under the frame of the room's wire wall.

"Git in here, little bit. You jus' a skinny little bit, you know dat?" He roughly drew her in with him, behind the shelves stacked with folded linens. "Yo' name Mahler, ain't it? Laney Mahler?"

She nodded, rubbing the arm he had released.

"Tha's too close to *my* name, *Marlin!* An' we cain't hab dat, das a bad situation! Lak, what jus' happen, Jack yellin' at you an' it was almos' lak he was yellin' at me! I'm chief, you know dat? Chief of the busboys! Ain't *nobody* yells at *me!*"

He stood taller, his brown face glistening with perspiration and wounded pride.

"Startin' rat now, you gonna have a new name. Yo' name gonna be 'Little Bit.' Got that? *Little Bit!* You jus' forgit your ol' name. Now, set down!" He seated her firmly on a wooden crate.

My men inside! They watched me dump a tray, and now they're eating their soup without biscuits!

Marlin had pulled over a stool and seated himself facing her. His long face was relaxing into its normal expression—solemn, with sloping, mournful-looking eyes.

"I'm sorry," she heard her voice say thinly, "about the mess in there."

Nodding, he dropped his chin and leaned closer, fixing her with his somber eyes. His voice softened. "Ah was jus' thinkin', now we got dat straighten' out, me an' you might set us up to go out, one of dese nights. Lak, a date. What you think of that?"

Laney sat paralyzed.

"How 'bout it, Little Bit? We could hab us a good time. Know what I mean?"

Still speechless, she stared at his large lips.

"Wha's a matter, you don' lak black boys?"

"I can't," she said. "I already have...someone else."

"A boyfrien'?" he gently intoned. "Where at?"

Unaccountably at such a time, sadness swept over her. "Well, he lives near my home. But he works here. As a bellhop."

"Hmm. Dat right? You gon' be seein' him here dis summer?"

"I don't think so. I wish...."

"Tch, tch," he clucked sadly.

"Marlin, please let me go!" she begged. "I'm in such trouble in there! Ronnie's going to kill me!"

Frowning in thought, he reached around to his hip pocket, drew out a wallet, and flipped it open. Holding it for her to see, he pointed to a photograph of an attractive black girl, standing with two braided and beribboned little girls.

"This here's my wife, Ginnie," he said, seemingly having dropped nearly all of his southern black slang. "And these are my two lil' girls, Shawna and Stephanie."

Laney nodded silently, finally unable to think at all.

"Now, get back to your job. An' do it right! Before Ronnie gets on you *good*!"

Laney scrambled out with her tray, ran for new biscuits, and hurried past the checker, who was busy and didn't look up. She knew that in the dining room, Ronnie might have taken over the table herself, or given it to another waitress. All possible situations awaiting her were horrific.

But she found her men peacefully finishing their soup— with biscuits. Patch was at their table, refilling their water glasses.

"Bless you, Patch!" Laney said.

"Where you been, dummy?" Patch asked. "Don't stop, keep goin'! Get your tail out to the range, you gotta pick up!"

Ronnie had appeared, so agitated that one curl was flopping loose. "You cause one more tray to fall and I'll *fire* you! Now, get out there for their entrées! Where's your check?"

"On the traystand," Laney muttered.

"Here!" Patched thrust it at her.

"On the *traystand?*" Ronnie's thick eyelashes rose in disbelief at this last stupidity of Laney's, getting separated from her check. Turning away, she marched off with an angry twitching of her hips.

"Jiggle, jiggle," Patch muttered, with her crooked jaw set nearly square. "Fat-assed Jezebel bitch!"

"Quiet, my men will hear you!"

"Git! Don't worry about your men," Patch said. "I'll fill 'em so full of water, they'll have to go to the john."

At the range, Laney collected her six entrées from Sterling, the cook, who gently advised her to be careful. She loaded them, three stacks of two each. Getting herself under the heavy tray, she hoisted it to her shoulder, deciding fingertips were unthinkable. Straightening, she balanced it on her flat palm and started out.

Before she reached the doors, suddenly the tray disappeared! Gone, the weight from her hand! While she stood dumbly, ahead of her ran a busboy—not Marlin, but one she didn't know—with her tray soaring high over his shoulder.

Why? Is he helping me?

She fluttered after him, weightless with fright, wondering if he would head for her station.

He did. After twirling the tray effortlessly down onto her traystand, he left without a backward glance, slipping like a black-and-white eel between the tables.

———

Laney cried quietly in bed that night, longing for home. She kept turning over, carefully, trying to keep her narrow bed from creaking.

I never thought I could get this homesick. Almost eighteen, and I'm acting like a big baby. I hate it here! This was all a terrible mistake. I know I could get my old job back....

The next morning, she sneaked along the outside wall of the help cafeteria to the rear, where there was a phone booth. Seldom used, it was full of dust and cobwebs.

But the phone worked. She laid out all of her dimes—five. "Hello, Mom?"

"Laney! Is that you? What is it? Is something wrong?"

"It's so good to hear your voice, Mother! No, nothing's wrong. I just wanted to talk a little...."

"Are you sure all's well, dear?" Vera asked. "You sound...I guess it's just being on long distance. You sound so far away."

"Well, I'm a little tired, I guess. It's...it's hard here, Mom. Harder than I thought it would be. And I miss you folks so much."

"My poor dear! We miss you, too. Reney goes into your room sometimes, and just lies on your bed. And I know how she feels."

Laney sniffled, and couldn't speak.

"Any sign yet of Jon Boyer?"

"No," she eked out. "Thank goodness."

"Let's pick a date for us to come there to see you. How about in two weeks or so? Could you see us that soon?"

"Yes. Yes, that would be good. Any day, actually. The sooner, the better!" Laney managed a small laugh, and her voice smoothed out as she explained her schedule. "I'll ask the hostess to make sure I work lunch. If I work dinner afterward, it's okay, as I have about three hours off in the afternoon. So come for lunch, and Dad can do his driving in daylight."

"That sounds perfect. I'm still looking forward to eating in that wonderful dining room! As soon as Harv gets home, I'll talk with him about it."

After they said goodbye and hung up, Laney lingered, thinking and wiping her wet cheeks. Her mother hadn't said what she'd hoped to hear, that she should quit at the hotel and come home. But the finality of her situation—knowing that she was there to stay, and had better get used to it—seemed oddly strengthening.

At dinner one evening shortly after this, Laney was returning from the kitchen with a tray load of soups and biscuits, glancing around for Hilda. Annoyingly, Hilda had started disappearing, even if they were busy. And now Laney saw that they had a new party. *How long have they been here?*

"Don't worry, I took their order," said Patch, glancing over her own loaded tables. "Want me to pick up their starts? Or want me to serve those soups, and you go?"

Laney thought fast. "Thanks, Patch. I'll go, if you'll serve the soups. Where the heck is Hilda?"

Patch handed her the new party's check. "She's out in the lounge with Ronnie, smoking."

"*Really!*"

"Ronnie'n her are old buddies, didn't you know?"

Laney, scowling, started out with her tray, when someone from behind touched her gently on the shoulder.

Turning, she looked up to see Jon Boyer. First startled by his bellhop's red and black uniform, she grew more surprised to see his face.

"Hello, Laney. I've caught up with you, finally."

She heard her voice, speaking: "Hi, Jon. It's good to see you." *That wonderful face! But he looks thinner, and tired. Maybe he's been sick.*

"It's wonderful to see you!" he said quietly. "Do you like it here so far?"

"Yes…pretty well. How's it going with you and Sheila? Are you married yet?"

He glanced away. "No. We've been engaged over a month, but it's not going well. That girl…." He shook his head dismally. "She doesn't know the meaning of compromise. The truth is, I'm afraid it's falling through, for us."

"Oh, no. I'm sorry to hear that."

"Thanks. If we do end it, and I'm pretty sure we will, would you like to see me again sometime? Maybe go out for a bite of dinner?"

Laney gazed at him. *He's asked me for a date!* It took a few seconds before she could make her stammering reply: "No, I don't think so…. No, I don't…. I'm sorry, but, no."

After an intense look at her, Jon turned bleakly away. Laney watched him leave, square shoulders in the perfectly-fitting red jacket swinging with less confidence than usual.

She glanced over her and Hilda's tables. Dimly, she recalled Patch silently taking her new check from her hand and leaving with it. The seated foursome were watching her. Hilda was approaching with a question on her face.

Laney stepped quickly to remove the foursome's soup bowls, and as Hilda was about to speak, started out for the kitchen. On the way, she passed Patch, returning with the starts; Patch gave her a curious look, but said nothing.

Away from them all, in the kitchen, she thought clearly enough to realize she'd finally had a chance, with Jon. *But how could he think I'd go out with him now? He can't be so dense he doesn't know what he did to me.*

That night, as she and Patch paused at the dorm before going their separate ways, Laney unburdened her mind, telling Patch the entire story.

Patch listened, at first enthralled to think of Laney falling from the school bus to practically land in Jon's arms. She was surprised to hear that, while he'd looked her up every time he came home, held her hands across the counter, and called her "his girl", they'd never actually had a date.

"What? I thought you was tellin' me you were sweethearts."

"I guess I was, and he wasn't."

"Well, you were a dupe, then."

"True. I was always hoping, and he was just stringing me along."

"Yep, you were a dupe, all right."

"I know I hurt him tonight. But *I* was *really* hurt when he jilted me, Patch."

The girl squared her jaw and thought a bit. "I'm not the guy to give advice, but I think you done the right thing."

"Thanks for that, Patch. I do, too."

———

The next day, after serving lunch, Laney and Patch went directly to the waitress lounge, where Danny had told them they could find Ronnie. They had decided to plead with her to make them partners in the dining room.

As they waited for Ronnie to appear, Laney asked Patch what her plans were for fall. "Are you saving money for college, or some other school, or what? You know I'll be going to a state teacher's college."

But Patch's face became glum, and she remained silent. Laney, surprised, was wondering if something was wrong, when Ronnie suddenly marched into the room, and the matter was dropped.

As the woman saw the two girls waiting, she took a lighter from her skirt pocket, and a cigarette. The girls waited patiently while she got it lit.

Finally she nodded through the smoke. Stating their case, sometimes both talking at once, the girls stacked up their reasons for wanting to be partners: they liked each other; Patch was experienced and could help Laney; they would work well together; they'd make a real team.

Patch pushed it further: "And I promise I'll behave myself."

Ronnie responded sourly: "That'll be the day." But in the end, she said that she had a new girl to work with Hilda, so she would permit the change.

They were partners! Their problems—Laney's lost love and Patch's uncertain plans for the future—were forgotten in a moment of relief and joy. Outside in the alley, they fell into step, arms around each other's waists, laughing and talking.

The very air seemed brighter, as the afternoon sun warmed the hillside above the alley, sending down the scent of young, green grass.

The real summer heat was still to come.

SECRETS TOLD AND SECRETS KEPT

The Vernal Springs Hotel Resort lay in early morning calm, with a slight mist rising from the dew-covered golf course, lawns, and famous rhododendrons: to preserve quiet for the sleeping guests, the grounds-keepers' lawnmowers were still silent. In the sprawling, main parking lot, only a limousine moved, nosing its way slowly between lines of cars toward the columned front entrance. Inside the hotel's dining room, no one yet stirred, although, in the large, high-raftered kitchen, cooks moved about with low voices and an occasional, muted clatter of pans.

While the hotel proper was largely asleep, the widened alley behind it was bustling. Two trucks maneuvered around each other, one bringing food to the kitchen's back entrance, the other hauling garbage out. Uniformed waitresses left their dormitory, calling to each other as they passed trucks and garbage bins, heading toward the employees' small cafeteria.

Laney Mahler had slept in—just a few minutes, but she hurried through the alley, tying her apron strings as she looked around for Patch, her recently-assigned partner in the dining room.

She approached the cafeteria unaware of a seeming miracle that had occurred inside; the five-gallon milk can, delivered there daily, had turned out to be pure cream. The room was filled with men's coarse talk and laughter, as workers who didn't ordinarily eat there stood around in bunches, drinking glasses of the thick, rich stuff.

Laney entered, baffled by the strange crowd, and picked up grapefruit and toast. Then, carrying her tray, she discovered the cream, and stood non-plussed. Glancing around, she located Patch, already seated and calmly pouring cream over cereal.

Patch spied her and called over, "Hurry up! I saved you a seat."

Laney greeted her, lowered her tray beside Patch's, and went back for cream. After pouring herself a cup nearly full, she topped it off with coffee. Then, back at the table, she drank it uneasily with her grapefruit, softening the dubious mix with toast. "This is going to curdle in my stomach," she muttered.

"Eat up, dummy," Patch said, working her slightly-crooked jaw as she chewed. "They're havin' turkey necks for lunch."

"Not again!" Laney moaned. "I hate them. They don't even taste like meat."

"I know. Prob'ly some of 'em ain't very fresh. I think the red stuff's supposed to cover up the taste, but it don't, quite." Her eyes twinkled. "A'course, you can just do like me—hold your nose and gulp it down." With short, brown hair and a face not quite symmetrical, Patch's eyes were her one beauty: a rich chestnut-brown, bespeaking her honesty and a hint of mischief.

While Laney was starting her first summer at the resort, Pat Church, who preferred the nickname, "Patch", was starting her third. Laney roomed upstairs in the shabby, paint-peeling dormitory, along with forty-seven other waitresses, but Patch lived below on the building's first floor, with her mother.

Laney, who had been curious about this, now asked, "Patch, why is your mother here? Does she work at the hotel, too?"

"Yep. She does the laundry for the dorm. Towels, bed-sheets, uniforms, and such. While you're out larkin' around, I'm down there ironin' uniforms."

Surprised, Laney fell silent. Then she mused, "I wondered what was on the first floor. So it's a laundry."

"We have big washers and dryers down there, behind our rooms. I sleep in the living room."

"We mostly iron our own uniforms, though, right?"

Patch corrected her: "Most girls pay *us* to iron 'em. Mom and me iron uniforms for a quarter each. I do a lot of 'em when I'm off work. You gonna have yours ironed?"

"No," Laney replied, "I think I'm going to need all my quarters. That's like one person's tip, in the dining room." Her goal for summer earnings, similar to that of other waitresses, was three hundred dollars, in this summer of 1952.

"What are you planning to do in the fall, Patch? I asked you before, remember? But you didn't say."

The girl thoughtfully chewed her toast for so long that Laney asked again: "Are you saving money for college, like me? Or some other kind of school?"

Patch rose quietly and picked up her tray. As she turned to leave, she grudgingly muttered, "I ain't sure yet what I'll be doin' this fall."

"You're not *sure* yet? It's getting pretty late!"

But Patch was heading for the door. Laney, still unanswered, quietly followed her out.

―∞―

In the hotel dining room, Ronnie, the hostess, had assigned the new partners a station of three four-seater tables and a deuce, or fourteen seats—a fair-sized station, for two eighteen-year-olds who served elegant dinners of five courses each. They alternated table service with "tray running"—bringing each course in from the kitchen on large, round trays which they carried by their right ear, on fingertips. The previous week, when Laney had first arrived, she had struggled to learn this skill, under the strict tutelage of Ronnie. Patch, with her two summers' previous experience, was an expert with the tray and all other aspects of the job.

As the girls entered the dining room, Laney looked to the front entrance for the morning flowers, and smiled. Sunlight streamed through the tall east windows, glowing on two large floral arrangements, this time mainly white peonies and tall, gold and coral gladiolas. For dinner, these would be replaced with flowers in rich reds and other, close colors, to go with scarlet menus—all part of the grandeur that awed and fascinated Laney. From hidden speakers, soft music now arose, Laney's favorite: an instrumental version of "Remember".

The girls checked their tables, refolding a napkin here, straightening a fork there, waiting for the front doors to open. Suddenly, the early morning calm was broken, as a squabble arose from nearby tables. Ronnie was loudly berating Ramona, a plump, sweet-faced waitress, about her appearance.

Ramona's tall partner, Kate, looked furious, with her hands on her hips. "What do you expect?" she shouted at Ronnie. "She just got up!"

"Well, roll her out earlier, then!" Ronnie's black curls bobbled atop her head. "She's gotta have time to dress herself right. Her shoes are dirty! And look at her hair!" Then, speaking to Ramona, "How long since you've even combed your hair?"

Ramona tearfully combed the somewhat matted curls with her fingers, as Kate retied her loose-hanging apron strings. "It's not that important, Ronnie," Kate muttered. "Leave us alone."

"I'll leave her alone—I'll kick her lazy backside out of the dorm!"

As Ronnie turned to leave, Kate stopped her with low, intensely spoken words: *"Just remember, if Ramona goes, I go."*

Ronnie opened her crimson mouth, then closed it tightly, and stalked off on her high, patent-leather heels.

"Ronnie's bein' her true self today," Patch flatly observed.

Laney was both shocked by the scene and impressed with Kate's courage. "How can Kate talk to Ronnie like that?" she asked.

"Simple. She knows Ronnie won't let her go. She's the best waitress here. Even Ramona ain't bad at table service. Ronnie gives 'em big parties, of eight or more. Ever notice Kate runnin' in with a heavy tray, and a busboy right behind her, carryin' another?"

"Yes," Laney replied thoughtfully, "I have seen that. And what is it with Kate, being so protective of Ramona?"

Patch nodded. "They were partners here last year, too. Kate says she likes Ramona 'cause Ramona don't give her any sass." She grinned wryly, and then added, "They been friends a long time, at home." Sobering, Patch lowered her voice. "And Kate's like that. She's just a real good person."

By then, the front doors had opened. Jack, the tuxedoed head waiter, hustled forward, bringing in the first party.

———⚬⚬⚬———

At dinner that evening, it was rumored that the crowd would be the largest yet this tourist season. Soon after the doors were opened, the two girls' station filled rapidly. Laney took orders from first two tables and started off with a tray, while Patch took the remaining orders and poured water.

Much later, after two of their full tables had been emptied and re-seated, Laney stood in a line of waitresses at the range, all pushing their trays along the steel ledge as they waited to pick up entrées.

A debacle had arisen, its cause unknown to Laney: a miscount could have occurred, creating a shortage of a particular entrée; orders could have been switched or confused; or, just the high demand might have caused the cooks to fall behind. Laney, anxious and perspiring, worried about Patch, in the dining room, with diners waiting for their food.

Two serving cooks at the counter were arguing, and, now, from behind a wall of steel shelves, the chefs started shouting and a plate landed with a crash.

Laney anxiously studied her two checks, feeling the first twinge of a headache.

Suddenly Patch appeared beside her, carrying another tray. "What's the holdup?"

"I don't know! What's happening with you? Is it rough in there?"

"Naw. It ain't bad. I'm pickin' up salads for the new foursome." Frowning, she peered closely at Laney. "Are you okay? Wanta trade places? You can pick up my salads and I'll wait here for your entrées."

"Bless you, Patch." Laney said ruefully. "No, I'll stay. We're moving a little, now."

"Okay. I'll tell our guys the cooks are fightin', that'll keep 'em quiet. Don't stew over it, Laney." Then she stalked off with her tray.

It was after ten o'clock when their last party had left, and they had reset their station for breakfast. As always, it was a pleasure and a relief to Laney to step outside into the alley's peaceful quiet. With the warm day's garbage smell abated, a faint honeysuckle scent was rising from a few vines at the foot of the hill. The air was warm and humid, the sky hazy with stars.

"It ain't a bad life, is it?" Patch asked, gazing upward as they sauntered toward the dorm.

"Not bad at all." Nearly worn out, Laney found she could still smile. "I'm sure glad I have you for a partner, Patch." She saw Patch, beside her, smiling in the alley's light.

Patch muttered shyly: "You're the best partner I ever had."

"Patch! How can you say that? You're the strong one!"

"Well, you're the pretty one. You'll bring in good tips."

Laney had to laugh. "Oh, baloney. Besides, we've got a long summer ahead. You might be changing your mind."

Patch's eyes widened: "Well, yeah…I *am* kinda concerned about *that!*"

Fridays were paydays in the dining room. At the end of the lunch shift, waitresses gathered at a window inside the kitchen to collect their slim pay envelopes. Hotel pay was meagre; the girls received most of their money from tips.

On Laney's second Friday, she collected her pay after Patch had already received hers and gone outside. Hurrying out, Laney saw her in the alley a short distance ahead. "Hey, Patch!" she called. "Wait a sec!"

Catching up to her, Laney found Patch looking away, trying to hide tears. "Oh, no," Laney breathed. "What's wrong?"

"Nothin'," Patch said, hastily wiping a cheek with her hand.

"C'mon, Patch! You can tell me! I tell you my troubles."

"I just had a fight with my mom. She made me give her all my money. She caught me before I could get it to Kate."

"To Kate? You give your money to Kate?"

"Shhh! Not so loud!" Patch sniffed and looked cautiously about. "Kate keeps it safe for me. I give Mom some tip money, but I hate it when she takes my whole pay envelope."

"My God!" Laney muttered. Walking, they had reached the dorm and didn't stop, but continued on up the alley. "Does she need the money?"

"I don't know," Patch said dejectedly. "I got two little brothers at home, but my dad and big brother work in the mines, and I don't think they need my money. An' I do! I earned it, an' I need it, if I'm ever gonna get an education."

"But…what about Kate and your money?"

"Kate hides it for me, in her room. *Don't tell anybody!* It's embarrassing as hell to me."

"You know I wouldn't! So you're saving for college, then?"

"Not college, nurse's training. There's a big, teaching hospital near here, in Fallsburg. I been hopin' for some time to go there, if I can scrape together the money."

"That's great, Patch! My sister's a nurse, and she loves it! How's it going, with the money? Do you think you'll have enough?"

"I doubt it," she replied glumly. "It's a big problem. I saved some money last winter, from ironing for a lady back home. But even with that, I prob'ly won't make it. I figure I'll be short at least a hundred bucks. I'm gonna make a real fool of myself, if I get registered and don't have enough money."

"Would you have to pay it all at once?" Laney asked.

"Yep. All of it, the first day. Five hundred bucks. You gotta pay for uniforms and books and such. Then the next two years are just three hundred each, 'cause by then you're workin' on the wards. I'd work holidays if I could, o' course, or any extra work I could get."

"Well," Laney said, speaking carefully, "did you ask if they have any help for girls who need money, like a loan or something?"

"I did, I asked about it when I sent in the application. But they sent me another letter sayin' I gotta pay all my first year's money up front."

"So you've already applied!" Laney exclaimed. "What does your mom think about all this?"

"Are you kiddin'? She hates it! She wants me to stay here an' help her! She don't even know I sent in the paper work. I had to send my high school record, too. If I'm accepted, I go in for an interview. I'm just waitin' to hear if I got accepted or not."

"Oh, my gosh! You must be watching the mail! Why didn't you tell me, Patch?"

Patch looked down, with no reply.

Laney didn't pursue it, asking instead, "Do you think your grades are good enough?"

"I don't know. They're 'bout average, I guess. I got A's in Home Ec and General Science, a couple others."

"Well, that's good. But…well, there's something I think I should mention, if you're going for an interview…." They stopped walking, and stood still. "It's not easy to say this."

"I know. Clean up my language. That's what Kate says."

"Watch your grammar," Laney said, "and don't say words like ain't, and hain't."

"I try, but it's hard. I keep forgettin'."

"Then I'll remind you," Laney promised. Having nearly reached the main road, they turned around wordlessly and started back to the dorm

———∞———

Before going to bed that night, Laney went searching for Kate, who slept in the room next to her own. There, she made her way to Kate's narrow bed among the fifteen other beds in the room. She asked her quietly to come out in the hall with her for a minute.

The puzzled Kate followed her out to the ironing board area, and they stood together in the light of a dim, bare bulb.

"I know about you keeping Patch's money for her," Laney began.

Kate frowned sharply. "Laney! Keep that quiet! Patch doesn't want it spread around!"

"Don't worry, I'll keep her secret," Laney assured her. "But I feel so bad for her. She wants to get into nurse's training. I guess you know about that."

Kate nodded her cropped-red head, glancing down the hall to where voices were quieting for the night. "Of course, I know. She's asked Danny to let her work all three shifts, but he won't let her. And that mother of hers…."

"Yes! What's the matter with her?"

"There are plenty of people like her. They think their kids owe them for having raised them, and when the kids grow up and start working, they should bring money into the home. People like that don't place much value on education."

Laney sighed sadly. "I guess maybe we could help her a little…."

"No. You and I need our money, too. I've put a little of my tip money in with hers, but not much. She's not dumb. And she won't accept help. She's made that clear to me."

"She has her pride," Laney said, nodding.

"Pride and shame, both," Kate added. "She's ashamed of the way her mother treats her."

Then they returned to their rooms, Kate to sleep and Laney to lie awake, thinking.

—◦◦◦—

In the dining room the next morning, Laney and Patch were serving breakfast, watching two ladies dawdle over their fruit parfaits, when Marlin, chief of the busboys, approached them. During Laney's first days there, working with Hilda, she had caused Marlin to drop a tray, and she hadn't forgotten his fury.

"Come 'long with me, Little Bit," Marlin now told her. "I gotta talk with you."

"What now?" she asked. After a quick look and a nod from Patch, she followed him.

He took her to the linen bin, a small, wire-walled enclosure off the kitchen. She followed him in, past shelves of folded linens.

Marlin's proud, brown face looked warily past her shoulder, as he drew her in a little further. "A friend o' mine'd like a date with you," he said. "Don't worry, he's a white guy. He's a stunt driver for Louie Atwood. You heard o' them, ain't you? Big outfit. They do shows at fairs an' things."

"Louie Atwood! Yes, of course, I've heard of them. They drive old rattletraps, and do dangerous tricks."

"Tha's right. He's good at it, though. He don't get hurt. His name's Tommy Dillon. So, how 'bout it? You interested in a date?"

Laney glanced out into the busy kitchen. "Gee, I don't know, Marlin. I don't know if I want to date anybody. And he doesn't sound like…like an ordinary guy. How old is he?"

"A lil' older'n you…, twenty, twenty-one." He grinned. "Funny, you don't ask if he's good-lookin'."

She shrugged. "That too, I guess."

"Yeah, he ain't too bad. He wanted me to set him up with a pretty girl here, and you da one." He followed this with a comical, toothy grin.

"Oh, Marlin." She sighed, and thought a bit. "It might be sort of nice to have a date. Maybe I could give it a try. Does he have a car?"

"He does. It's a beaut. He said somethin' about a movie in Fallsburg."

Laney nodded. "Well, I wouldn't mind a movie. Okay. I guess you can tell him I'll go out with him."

Saturday night was always special in the waitress dormitory, for no good reason; what had been date night in high school was just another night, behind the hotel. Seldom did any girl have an actual date. An aura of loneliness, or longing, hung in the air. Some of the girls gathered outside the cafeteria in the alley lights to talk and visit. Others stayed in their rooms, studying their movie magazines and listening to radio songs about love and broken hearts.

At seven o'clock, Laney waited on the dorm porch for the "beaut" of a car to arrive. A breeze from the hillside above brought the summery smell of drying grass, while a thin, pale slice of July moon sailed high over the alley. Laney felt a brief longing for her old boyfriend, Jon. With Patch's problems having driven high school memories out of her mind, this soft, warm night was working it's spell; she was a young, wistful girl again.

A group of waitresses who apparently had dinner off were already gathered in the alley, talking and laughing. Laney gave them a small wave, but remained where she was, feeling awkwardly separated from them.

Soon, a shiny, new, red-and-white Buick slowed gently to a stop near the porch. With its approach, all talk in the alley stopped.

The driver's door opened, and a young man came striding past the front of the car. Laney's initial reaction was disappointment—he was only slightly taller than her five-foot-three, with longish, glistening hair swept back from a rough-looking forehead.

As he held out his hand, his smile widened happily to see her. "You look wonderful, Laney."

She took his hand without looking too closely at his face, reminding herself that looks didn't really matter.

"Thank you," she said, and then, because it seemed necessary, she added, "So do you." *Here I go, starting out with a lie.*

Taking her gingerly by the elbow, he led her to the car, which gleamed in the twilight. She slid onto the seat and ran her hand over its smooth leather surface. Even the dashboard seemed to be covered with leather.

"I see you like my car. It's a Roadmaster Riviera," he said proudly, as he threw an arm over the seat to look back, then executed a perfect U-turn. "Just three more payments, and she's mine."

Tommy smelled like Old Spice, which Laney loved. She wondered if she could possibly like him, after all.

"It's beautiful!" she said. "It's the nicest car I've ever been inside."

He shot her a pleased look. "You're what?" he asked. "Eighteen or so?"

"I just lately turned eighteen," she said. "And could I ask, how old are you?"

"Well, yes, I'm twenty…one."

He stumbled slightly over the words. She suspected that he was fibbing: he seemed older, even though he was a slight man, thin to the point of being scrawny.

"And you have such an exciting job!" she said. "Or is it not exactly a job?"

He gave a short, barking laugh. "Job, vocation…. It's more like a hobby than anything. You have to love danger, to jump those cars and run on two wheels…, stuff like that. And it pays damn good money." Steering hand-over-hand, he turned onto the main highway. Then he asked, "You dating anyone else right now?"

"No," she answered. "I dated a few boys in high school. But none of them steady. Mostly I was just too busy."

"Oh?" he said. "Doing what?"

"I worked in a drugstore part-time, and I played the organ for church. Choir practices and such, at night. So I didn't have many free evenings."

Tommy's eyes turned toward her and lingered briefly on her face. Then he drove on in silence. It occurred to Laney that he was disappointed to hear about her prosaic-sounding life.

During the movie, with Old Spice floating in the darkness, Laney sat in the curve of his arm stretched around her shoulders. Occasionally he moved his head closer to hers and gave her shoulders a squeeze. He felt slightly damp, and this closeness became increasingly uncomfortable. But, rather than risk offending him, she sat still and remained silent.

After they finally left the theater, Tommy drove them to a drugstore, where they drank milkshakes—not as thick and chocolatey as the ones she had made in the drugstore, but still enjoyable. While they sipped, he talked nonstop about driving stunt cars.

"Balancing on two wheels is nothing much," he said. "All that can happen is you'll flop over, and anyway, you're strapped in. It's the ramps, and jumpin' cars, that's the killer. And I happen to be good at it. It's a little scary when you're flyin'up there and seeing air, then it's Kablamm! and you're on the ground—*hopefully,* you made it over one or two of them babies, and you're on the ground."

Laney watched, mesmerized, briefly caught up in his excitement. Meanwhile, she had a full view of his face. He definitely had acne. He had smoothed it somewhat with a pinkish lotion or cream that had dried chalky-looking. With mild sympathy, she saw that he knew it looked bad and was trying his best to do something about it.

"I think it must take courage," she said.

"Yessir, it's a dangerous life I lead," Tommy said. "It's worth it, though. I really like it."

Watching his light blue eyes as they shifted around the room, she wondered if he was ever afraid.

When they arrived back in the alley, he stopped the car a short distance before reaching the dorm. In the alley lights ahead of them, Laney could see his pale face. She waited apprehensively while he turned off the engine. Then he slid over on the wide seat to get closer. Without a word, he drew her close and started kissing her on the lips.

Repulsed by his wet, sour-milkshake mouth, she decided she could endure it a short while. But he soon started climbing over the gearshift to get even closer. In what seemed like a practiced move, suddenly his hands were tugging at her blouse, pulling it free of her skirt. Then his hands were inside the blouse.

At first shocked, Laney came to quickly as it became a battle. Drawing her face free of his, she started fighting off his hands.

"What's the matter?" he asked.

"I'm not used to heavy necking like this, Tommy. It's a first date, and we hardly know each other, and—"

"So what? Does it matter? Most of the girls I date don't care."

"Well, I do. I guess my experience has been different from yours." She inched away and started re-tucking her blouse.

Blowing out a disgusted sigh, he slid back under the wheel. As he started the car and drove forward to the dorm, Laney glanced up to the lit windows above, where a few heads had appeared, looking down.

The car eased to a stop. As Laney climbed out, Tommy hurried around the car to meet her on the porch. In full view of the watchers, Laney submitted to one last kiss.

As they said goodnight, Laney thanked him dully for the movie and the milkshake. But she didn't tell him she'd had a wonderful time.

The next morning she described the date to Patch, in the cafeteria. "He was trying to get inside my clothes! We almost had a battle, in the car! And on the first date!" Then she added, with a grin, "Besides, he was a terrible kisser."

Patch chortled, showing no trace of sympathy. "I had a boyfriend, once," she divulged, "till he moved away. Me and him had some good times together."

"That's *he and I*," Laney interjected quietly. "He and I had some good times together."

"Well, yeah, *he and I*. Anyway, I didn't care much for his lovemakin', either. He was so dumb and awkward, he actu'lly clipped me on the jaw, once. That's why it's crooked."

"Oh, Patch," Laney scoffed, laughing.

"I just mostly liked him 'cause he could skip a stone six times across the river."

In the dining room, Ronnie added a deuce and a foursome to their station, increasing it from fourteen to twenty diners. As they became more proficient, they developed systems for sharing the work, moving smoothly and quietly, often communicating with each other using little more than nods and glances.

At breakfast on an early July morning, Laney was watching the kitchen's swinging doors, where a roommate of hers had just dropped a tray. While the girl was being rudely dispatched by Jack, two busboys cleared away the mess, with the other door propped open for two-way traffic. While Laney watched, Kate suddenly came hustling through the open door.

As her eyes located Patch and Laney, she raised a hand straight up and hurried toward them.

"What's happening?" Patch asked.

The redhead glanced around to make sure no one was watching. Then she drew a long envelope just far enough from her wide, apron pocket that Patch could see it, and pushed it back out of sight again.

"Mail," Kate said quietly. "I grabbed this for you, Patch. It's from the hospital."

"Oh, no!" Patch said. She stared into space, wide-eyed. "I don't wanna read it right now. Just stick it in my apron."

Kate surreptitiously transferred the envelope to Patch's pocket.

"I really 'preciate you girls helpin' me with all this," Patch said. "You must think I'm a reg'lar pain in the neck."

"Yes, I think so, don't you Kate?" Laney asked casually.

"I think she's more of a pain somewhere else," the redhead replied.

"Thanks a lot." Patch wasn't smiling. "Well, this letter could be the end of my plans. I kinda hope it is."

Laney quickly changed her tune: "Patch! I hope not!"

"Don't start thinking like that, now," Kate scolded, then rushed off to her station, where Ramona was alone.

Back to work again, Patch asked to run the next tray, saying she needed to "work off her nerves". But Laney urged her to just leave, and read her letter. Patch finally agreed, slinking away as if anticipating the worst news.

After finishing breakfast alone, Laney hurried out into the hot alley, where she found Patch, Kate, and Ramona waiting in the cafeteria's narrow strip of shade. Laney looked to Patch for a clue, but her pale face revealed nothing—neither success nor failure.

As Laney joined them, Patch said joylessly, "I got my interview. It's Friday, August the fifth. So my grades must'a been okay. I guess I should be happy. I am, sort of."

Then, as Laney whooped and threw her arms around her, Patch finally had to break out laughing. "Stop it, will ya?" she begged. "You don't hafta throw a fit!"

Gradually they settled themselves, and made their way, with hushed voices, into the cafeteria.

As they sat together at a back table, Patch ate little, mainly just staring at her plate. "Now I better get on the ball. I gotta work on my terrible English."

Ramona looked up over her soup. "Your English isn't so bad, Patch. I think they'll take you just the way you are. You're a very nice girl."

"I think," Laney said solemnly, "your best bet is just to be your true, honest self."

And Kate concurred, adding, "But watch your grammar."

On the way to the dorm, Patch confided to Laney, "The truth is, my brain's in such a muddle, I can't think straight. What if I pass the interview? It ain't likely, but then, I didn't really think I'd get this far. What if I do pass, and can't afford to go?"

"I know, Patch," Laney said sadly. "I don't know what to say. I guess you'll just have to take it one step at a time."

———

In late July, when Laney's family arrived for their promised visit, Laney introduced the shy, awkward Patch to them at lunch in the dining room. Saying little, Patch spooned out Vera Mahler's creamy casserole like the true professional that she was. Then Patch insisted on serving the remainder of the lunch herself, so Laney could leave and visit with her folks. After a brief tour of the dormitory, Laney lead her parents to a quiet, back corner of the cafeteria for coffee and talk.

First glancing around to ensure their privacy, she confided to them Patch's wishful plans for nurses' training, and her money problem. "She expects to be short about a hundred dollars, and time is running out."

Vera mulled it over. "Is there any extra work she could do here at the hotel?"

"No, unfortunately. She has asked Danny to let her work all three meals, but he won't allow it. She irons a lot of waitress uniforms—the girls pay a quarter per uniform—but her mom doesn't let her keep the money. And she won't help pay for Patch's education. It's a bad situation; her mother doesn't want her to leave and become a nurse."

Harv, who had been smilingly watching Laney's face, now spoke up. "That's a shame. The woman had better look to the girl's future."

Vera said wonderingly, "Could the other waitresses help her out? If they each gave a dollar or two.... There are so many girls."

"I know. They'd do it, too, I'll bet." Laney grew thoughtful. "The problem is, though, Patch is too proud. She has warned me and another friend, Kate, not to try and give her money, because she won't accept it."

Vera nodded sympathetically. "Yes, that would be embarrassing, taking money from your friends. It would sort of take away your pride. I'm sorry I can't help you, Laney. That's a tough situation."

———

After her family had left, Laney returned to the dorm. She climbed the stairs slowly, ascending into the upstairs's increasing heat. In her room, she removed her apron and lingered, briefly. Then she hurried next-door to Kate's room.

She found the girl lounging on her bed in her underwear, reading a magazine. Near her, girls laughed and chattered. Bending down to her, Laney quietly asked her to come out to the ironing boards, again.

A sharp look from Kate said, what now? But she checked her watch, swung her long legs off the bed, and followed Laney out.

"I think I'm getting an idea for how to help Patch with money," Laney began.

"You think you're getting an idea," Kate said sarcastically. "Great."

"How many girls are in the dorm, about fifty?"

Kate thought quickly. "There are forty-nine waitresses. Not counting Patch, there'd be forty-eight, up here. So?"

"What if each girl donated two dollars for Patch?" Laney asked. "See how easy it would be to raise a hundred bucks? I think the girls would do it gladly. Patch is well-liked, you know."

"What are you talking about? The girls don't know anything about her situation!"

"I know that, Kate. We'd have to tell them. We'd have to hold a meeting, up here, and ask for their help."

"*What*? When Patch is so secretive about it? We can't just open it up to everybody!"

This notion struck Laney from a new angle, giving her pause. Then she ventured, "But if she didn't know what we were doing...."

"How would we ever keep it a secret? Forty-eight girls, keeping a secret from Patch?"

"Well...," Laney began again, but tapered off.

"Besides, even if we got the money, Patch would never accept it. How would you plan to get around that?"

Then they parted. Kate left in a huff to don her dinner uniform while Laney remained there, gazing down the stairs to the alley's bright glare, seeing her wishful plan evaporate away in the heat.

⸻

Each day, Laney and Patch managed their large station with improved skills. Once Ronnie stopped by to look over their tables and gave the girls an approving nod. Her gesture gave Laney a lift, seeming to speak high praise. But Patch expressed her typical opinion: "She ain't about to praise us, especially not me."

"She *isn't* about to, Patch. Not ain't."

"Oh, right, *isn't*. Sorry. She isn't about to do anything nice, for me."

Patch seemed to Laney as strong as a horse, gliding along with scarcely a ripple beneath heavy trays. Laney also had become skillful, swinging along gracefully and lowering her tray to the stand with a perfect twirl. Patch seemed to find time to help any waitress around them who needed help—pouring water here, clearing a table there—waving off thanks, and always with her quick and mildly subversive wit.

August brought conventions to the hotel, with each organization filling the dining room nearly to capacity. Rather than trickling in, the diners arrived all at once. A big help for the waitresses was having a set menu, usually with guests having a choice between two entrées.

On one convention evening, the dining room's air conditioning failed. Waiting for the diners to pour in, Patch and Laney sipped ice water, while Ramona, a few tables over, drew her apron up to wipe her face. Later, that suffering girl opened the dining room's wide, heavy silverware drawer, and accidentally pulled it out all the way, where it fell with the sound of a car crash. In the steamy kitchen, confusion over an order caused the serving cooks to shout at a girl, who ran out crying. Laney and Patch worked steadily through it all, knowing their roles so well, there was little need for talk.

It was nearly eleven o'clock when the conventioneers, who had all arrived at once, trickled out with maddening slowness. At last Laney and Patch could reset their station for breakfast, and were free to leave. But as they headed through the kitchen, they were stopped by Marlin, who came running up behind them.

"Hup hup! Little Bit! Wait up!"

Laney stopped resignedly, waving Patch on.

Marlin looked exhausted, his white jacket spotted with food and his dark face glistening with sweat.

"Hello, Marlin. Long night, wasn't it?"

"Dang long. Listen, I got bad news. Tommy Dillon hurt hisself in a car crash las' week. He says he was cut up some. But he's better now, and he wants to see you again. The poor guy needs some cheerin' up. Can I set a date for him 'n you?"

Laney paused. Briefly the quiet, late-hour kitchen seemed whirling around her. "Marlin, I'm sorry, but I didn't even like the guy. He's too fresh, and he's just not my type. I don't want to date him again."

The haggard youth's shoulders drooped further. "Dang it, I can't believe dis, Little Bit. Ain't you got no heart? The guy's had a lotta pain. He had to get sewed up in the hospital and stay overnight. He's lost his bran' new car, and he hadn' even insured it yet."

"You mean, he didn't crash a stunt car?"

"No! He was drivin' *his* car, an' some drunken fool ran him off the road!"

"Oh, no! His beautiful car!" Laney's weary brain rose up in pity.

"How 'bout it? Can we make it Saturday night again? 'Bout seven?"

"Well…." She sighed wearily. "I'm too tired to even think about it. I'll let you know in a day or two, alright?"

He agreed reluctantly. "Don' wait too long."

After taking a few steps away, Laney stopped short and turned around. "Marlin! Wait! I want to settle it now."

"Good. You made up your mind."

"Yes. There's no use stringing you along. I'm sorry, but I really don't want to see him again."

"Now, wait a minute!"

"I'm sorry for him—you can tell him that. But I don't think I should have to go out with him, if I don't want to."

Marlin's jaw dropped as she went on: "Why do you keep setting up dates for him? Can't he get his own girls?"

"You kiddin'? The way that guy looks?"

"But, why do you do it?"

Marlin sighed heavily, glancing away. "He lent me money once, a while back, when I didn' have nothin' and nobody else would give me a dime."

"Did you ever pay him back?"

"Course I did. What'ta'ya take me for?"

"Well…." She paused, stymied. "So you do him this favor out of friendship? That's nice of you, Marlin, to help a friend. But, it's still 'No'. He isn't a friend of mine."

He stared at her wordlessly as she turned to go. "Good night, Marlin. I'm really tired, and I'm leaving."

She glanced back once to see him wearily turning away.

In the dorm, she climbed into bed just as the nightly dimming of alley lights below cast the room into deeper darkness. *Now I'm going to feel awful for what I did, refusing to date the poor guy while he's suffering.*

But, surprisingly, the next thing she knew, it was morning.

In late July, Patch told Ronnie that she'd need to be excused from work on August fifth, for her interview at the hospital. She also hinted strongly that it would be helpful if either Laney or Kate, or both, could accompany her on the fearsome trip.

Ronnie made the decision: Kate would be freed to accompany Patch, leaving Ramona and Laney to work one station. The four girls were agreeable to the plan—especially Ramona, who liked the idea of working with Laney.

When August fifth arrived, Laney and Ramona waved goodbye in the alley as the taxi pulled out, bearing Patch and Kate on their way to Fallsburg. Then they turned reluctantly to their much less interesting day, in the dining room.

As they worked breakfast together, Patch's plight was never far from Laney's mind. But fleeting thoughts were all she had time for; the gentle, smiling Ramona didn't hold up her end. Not only did Laney run the trays—she also did most of the table work. Her appreciation grew for Kate, who covered and filled in for her weaker partner without complaint.

When the long morning was past, the two of them hurried out to the alley. They had just a few minutes' wait before the taxi nosed past the corner of the dorm.

The back door opened; Kate was first to climb out. Seeing the two girls, she gave them a jubilant smile and a thumbs-up, while Patch paid the driver. Laney and Ramona rushed out to them, shouting.

Turning to them, Patch's face lit up in its crooked grin. "I made it! I actually passed the interview." Then she had to scold: "Hush up, will ya? You're doin' it again! Don't get people runnin' out to see what's goin' on."

Quieting down, they trooped into the cafeteria where, at a back table, Patch quietly described her day. "I tried to speak well, but I had to correct myself a couple times. Then I remembered what you said 'bout just bein' honest. I told Mrs. Johnson I knew I had a problem, but I was workin' on it. And she said I got a A for effort. Jeez, I still can't believe it! She was *nice*! And now I just have to show up, the Thursday after Labor Day."

After they celebrated with soup and buttered crackers, they returned to the dorm. Kate and Ramona plodded up the stairs, while Patch and Laney lingered on the porch.

"How did it go for you," Patch asked, "working with Ramona?"

Laney made a sour face. "I really missed you, Patch."

Her partner grinned. "Good. I'm glad you had it rough."

"Thanks a lot. Anyway, I'm happy for you. Things are going your way, Patch."

"It's like you said, one step at a time. I feel kind of strange right now. It's like, all this crazy happiness when I know I'm soon gonna step off a cliff."

"Patch! Don't think such things! Hang on, something could still turn up. Darn it, I wish there were something I could do."

"Well, there ain't. Isn't. It's my problem. I appreciate you caring about it, and all. But there's nothing you, or Kate, or anybody else can do to help me."

—∞∞—

After working lunch the next day, Laney and Patch parted at the dorm, as usual, to go their separate ways. Laney waited upstairs in her room for a few minutes. Then, making sure that Patch was out of sight, she returned to the hotel kitchen. There she spoke to the people in the salad area, and begged from them a large mayonnaise jar.

She quickly sneaked the jar into the dorm and carried it into Kate's room. Only a few other girls were there, talking quietly. The redhead sat on her bed, bent over a small radio.

"Get up, Kate," Laney said quietly. "We need to talk, again."

Kate scowled, but got up and followed her out. "I can't believe you're still scheming," she muttered in the hall. "You're living on smoke and dreams."

"No, I'm not. I *was* living on smoke and dreams. Now I'm going to do something about it." She held up the glass jar.

"Don't tell me! You're actually going to ask the girls for money?"

"I am," Laney affirmed. "I'm pretty sure they'll give it. Some might even give more than two bucks."

"And they're all going to keep it a secret, right? That's the catch, Laney."

"I don't think so. I think when they realize how important it is, they'll keep it quiet. Remember surprise birthday parties, Kate? How do they keep them a secret?"

Kate paused, briefly. Then she said, "I trust you've also planned how to give the money to Patch?"

"Not quite. I've considered just mailing it to her, but I'm afraid she'd smell a rat. Or two rats—you and me. And we'd have to lie to her. But it's getting late; we have, what, ten days? We need to tell the girls about it now!"

"You mean, *right now?*"

"Let's do it tonight. We'll have to get them all together. How about at ten o'clock?"

"God, Laney! Wait a minute! "

"Let's meet in your room. It's bigger than mine. It'll be crowded, but girls can sit on the beds."

This time Kate paused, and Laney sensed she was wavering. "I wonder," Kate said musingly, "if this could possibly work." She shook her head dolefully. Then she stopped, and seemed to have made a decision. "If we have this meeting, you'll do all the talking, right?"

"I will," said Laney. "You can pitch in if you want to. We can do this, Kate. We have to have a little confidence in ourselves."

Laney turned away and started slowly down the hall, planning what she would say. Then she speeded up. In each room, she made her announcement to the girls who were there, about a secret meeting to be held at ten o'clock that night, in Kate's room. She stressed it being a *secret* meeting, with not a word to be said about it outside the dorm. After dinner, they were to quietly inform roommates who were not there now.

While the night air cooled slightly in the alley, it brought little relief to the dorm, where the upper floor was like an oven. In Kate's room, windows were open to catch the faintest breeze, as forty-six girls sat or sprawled on the beds in their thin night-gowns or pajamas. Some fanned themselves with magazines.

Laney tried to quiet the girls, who were more ready for a little bedtime fun than for anything serious. She was thankful for Kate's presence, the redhead being not only older than most of the girls, but also taller and louder. When Kate called them to order, they calmed down and listened.

Laney started by describing Patch's situation: she had passed all the requirements to enter nurse's training this fall, but didn't have enough money to pay for it. Even after working the Labor Day weekend, she would be short about a hundred dollars. Her mother wanted to keep her here, working in the laundry, and refused to help her. If something didn't turn up, Patch's hopes and plans for nurse's training would fall apart.

To the roomful of girls, all this came as a surprise. Laney explained that Patch had kept her problems mainly to herself, because she was embarrassed about her predicament. Heads nodded and a sympathetic murmur arose: yes, they could understand that.

Quiet conversations about Mrs. Church began, one girl observing aloud that she wasn't friendly with the girls.

Another added, "She looks like an ogre."

"Wait a minute!" A short blond spoke up: "We pay to have uniforms ironed, and I think Patch irons in her time off. She should be making pretty good money."

"The trouble is," Laney explained, "she doesn't get to *keep* that money."

This quieted the blond, and the whole room: Patch's situation was worse than they had first thought.

Kate finally spoke up. "There's forty-eight of us up here. If we each donated two bucks, we'd have almost the whole hundred. I know we all need our money. But if you could spare it, we could actually solve Patch's problem."

A few heads slowly nodded, though the group as a whole remained quiet and thoughtful.

Finally, someone said, "What a nasty break for her! She's even registered, and everything!"

Then another voice: "If there's anyone who deserves a chance, it's Patch. That girl has helped me in the dining room so many times...."

"I think I'll start ironing my own uniforms," an older girls said, "and give Patch the money. I should have been ironing them all along."

"I could iron eight of mine," said another, "and give her the quarters."

Laney addressed them all again: "There's one very important thing. We have got to keep this a secret from Patch. We can't discuss it anywhere but here in our rooms. Patch has a lot of pride. If she catches wind of this, she'll be humiliated.

Then everything will fall through, because she won't accept the money."

"I tried to share my tips with her, a little bit," Kate added. "But she told me not to try and give her money, because she won't take it."

"Wow, this is going to be tough," someone said.

"It won't be easy," Kate agreed.

It took several seconds for the seriousness of the problem to sink in throughout the room.

Then Laney spoke up: "I don't know about the rest of you, but, for Patch, I can keep my mouth shut."

"So can I," said another girl. "We just have to keep our wits about us."

"No talking about it anywhere but *right here*."

Then there was an air of muted excitement, as the girls parted and returned to their rooms. Keeping an important secret had united them, all girls fully involved. With their minds set on secrecy, their voices were already hushed.

Before going to bed, Laney used a lipstick to print "For Patch" on the side of the mayonnaise jar. She dropped her two dollars in. Then she placed the jar on a shelf in her room, on the wall nearest the ironing boards.

The following day, someone with a different lipstick printed below Laney's lettering, "Keep the secret!"

More dollar bills and change appeared in the jar.

Shortly after that, someone tacked up beside it a World War II poster she had brought from home, showing a battleship plunging through ocean waves. The poster's heading read, "Loose Lips Sink Ships." The girls laughed at it, but all agreed that it was relevant.

∞

Late the following evening, after Laney and Patch had nearly finished serving dinner, they were looking forward to going back to their rooms and collapsing. Laney was in the kitchen, picking up desserts for their last foursome, when Patch appeared beside her with another tray.

"Guess what?" Patch muttered. "We got a new party."

"No! The dining room should be closed by now!"

"This one's special. It's just one guy, and he's asking for you."

"Asking for *me*?"

"Yep. Jack brought him to our station. He's sittin' in there now. I'm picking up his starts."

"Just one guy? Oh, no! Oh, my God!" Laney had to correct her grip on the tray of desserts. "It's Tommy! It's got to be Tommy!"

"You mean, your horrible date?" asked Patch. "I don't think so. This guy ain't all that bad lookin'."

"It couldn't be Jon, eating here. Who else could it be? What color's his hair?"

"Well…, brown."

"Patch," she cried, "I can't face him again! You've got to help me!"

Patch deliberated. "Don't have a conniption fit. I told him I'd come out here and fetch you. I could tell him I didn't know it, but you already left for the night."

"That's perfect! Would you? I'd be so grateful! You'd have to finish in there without me...."

"It's nothin', just the last foursome and that guy. I'll take your desserts in with his crab cocktail. Go on, go. If he gets smart with me, I'll pour cocktail sauce down his neck."

After transferring the man's appetizer to Laney's dessert tray, Patch hoisted it to her fingertips and tramped off with it.

Then Laney crept uneasily out into the night.

The following day, after the lunch shift, she was due for another surprise. She was leaving the dining room, trailing behind Patch, when she was stopped by Danny Joyce, the maître d', who was standing outside the lounge. He surprised her by taking hold of her arm, while keeping his eyes on Patch until the girl had disappeared through the swinging doors.

"What is it?" Laney asked, with her heart thumping.

Danny drew her into the lounge. "Good things. All good things, Laney. Come here, Sweetheart. How are you?" Danny, who had a reputation for putting his hands on the waitresses, had gotten uncomfortably close to Laney during her job interview. But since then, she had received nothing from him except occasional greetings, sometimes with a friendly squeeze.

Now he glanced around. Two waitresses, who had been chatting nearby, were just leaving.

"I want to talk to you," he said to Laney, "about what you're doing for Patch."

Laney's hand flew to her lips. "Oh, no! How did you find out about it? We're trying so hard to keep it a secret!"

"Shhh. Say no more." Then he spoke sternly. "I like to know what goes on around here, Laney. I was told about it by Ronnie. She was on the stairs in the dorm and heard the girls above her talking."

"Well, what…, are you angry? Is it wrong? Do we have to stop?"

"No, you do not. Keep right on. It's a good thing. What I want to do—" he paused to draw a wallet from his hip pocket—"is donate to the cause. Patch is a good girl, and her mother doesn't deserve her." He opened the wallet and drew from it three five-dollar bills, which he thrust into Laney's hands.

"Fifteen dollars! Oh, thank you, Danny!" She spread them out happily in her hands.

He was now reaching into his front pants pocket, from which he drew another five. "And this is from Ronnie."

"Ronnie wants to help us?" Instantly she regretted sounding so surprised.

"Yes, she does. She's not a bad person, Laney."

"Wow! I guess not! How can we ever thank her? And you? Especially you!"

Without so much as a glance at the open doorway, he drew her close, held her face in his hands, and kissed her warmly on the lips.

Then she was released, feeling flushed and shaken.

When she walked out through the kitchen, she had her half of the meal's tips in her apron pocket—plus an extra twenty dollars. *That was the nicest kiss I've ever had*, she thought with amazement. Then she had to grin. *Now I'm taking money for sex.*

"Hello, Mom! It's me, Laney." She was speaking again on the alley phone.

Vera answered: "I thought maybe you'd call today! How are you? Are you winding up things there?"

"Am I! You wouldn't believe how busy I am. The waitresses are collecting money for Patch, like we talked about, Mother. Two dollars per girl. I think we're going to have enough!"

"That's wonderful! You're actually doing it! Dad and I could contribute a little…."

"No, thanks, Mom, we won't need it. You'll be here too late, anyway."

They made plans to pick up Laney at the dorm the day following Labor Day. Then, as they were ending their conversation, Vera's voice brightened.

"Oh, Laney, I almost forgot! I have good news for you! Do you remember your very first date, with Jimmy Bowman?"

"The bike rider! Yes, I remember him. That was so long ago. I was fourteen…."

"He came to our front door lately, asking for you! He and his mother have moved back to town. He'll be entering the teacher's college, along with you!"

"Really? Great! I liked him. He was a nice little guy." Then the thought struck her: "Mom, did you by chance tell him where I am?"

"Of course. Why wouldn't I? He was planning to come over there one evening and have dinner."

"Is that right? Oh, my gosh!" Laney had a laugh ready, but stopped herself; she would save that good story for later.

"You may not recognize him now," Vera said. "He must be six feet tall."

As they said their good-byes, Laney was distracted, her thoughts caught on her mother's last words. *Jimmy was six feet tall?*

She smiled, hurrying back to the dorm. It felt so good to have something to be happy about that she laughed quietly as she jogged up the stairs.

Hurrying into her room, she first checked the money jar. Yes; as always, it seemed to contain more bills, and change.

But what would they do with the money? How could they give it to Patch? Her brief joy hadn't lasted long; it was fading already, as she donned her white uniform for dinner.

The Tuesday before Labor Day, Kate dumped all the dollar bills and change in the glass jar out onto her bed, where she and two other girls counted it. After the contributions from Danny and Ronnie, the amount totaled one hundred eleven dollars and seventy-five cents, to which Kate had promptly added a quarter, making it one hundred and twelve.

Laney lay awake that night, thinking, long after the dorm had grown dark and still. Then she got up quietly and crept into Kate's room again. Careful not to bump any of the other beds, she bent over the sleeping girl.

"Kate! Wake up!" she whispered, gently shaking the girl. "It's me."

Kate stirred, and grumbled. "What now?"

"Shhh. Come on out, will you? I've got it all figured out."

Kate sat up, drooping, and sighed wearily. Then she rose, wrapped some garment over her underwear, and followed Laney out of the room.

"I've decided who can give the money to Patch," Laney said quietly. "There's only one person she would accept it from."

Kate's eyes showed their whites in the dim light. "Who?"

"Her mother."

Kate drew back. "Her *mother?*"

"Shhh! In spite of everything," Laney went on, "she is Patch's mom. I can't believe there's a mother anywhere who doesn't love her daughter. We can tell her how everyone likes Patch and respects her. And tell her she should be proud of her."

Kate's voice grew more incredulous. "And you think that will sway her? I can't believe this!"

"Then we'll tell her we learned that Patch needs a hundred dollars for nurse's training, so we decided to each donate a little. We're asking her to give it to Patch, and not say where it came from, because Patch wouldn't accept it from us. She must say it's a gift from herself."

"Stop it, Laney! This is craziness!"

"Wait. There's more. We have a clincher. We can tell her that Danny Joyce approves of our plan. He's even contributed money to it."

Kate opened her mouth to protest again, but remained silent.

"Do you get that, Kate? Danny knows about it. He's involved in it. She'll have no choice but to give Patch the money." While Kate remained speechless, Laney went on: "We'll just have to make sure she tells Patch that the money is from her, and not from us."

In mid-morning the next day, after the breakfast shift, Kate and Laney met once more in Kate's room with all available waitresses. They told the girls about Danny's and Ronnie's donated money, and the grand total in the jar of a hundred and twelve dollars.

The girls started up a happy shout, but Kate quickly quieted them down.

Then Laney told them the plan. They would ask Mrs. Church to give Patch the money, saying that it was a gift from herself. Despite the woman's attitude about money, Laney explained, she surely loved her daughter. Also, she should be strongly influenced by knowing that Danny Joyce was involved.

"But after Mrs. Church gives her the money," Laney continued, "remember, we mustn't rush to congratulate Patch, because we're not supposed to know anything about it. *We can't even know how it turns out unless Patch tells us.*"

Her words brought complete silence to the room.

Kate spoke next. "It could be that Patch gets the money, but doesn't tell any of us. That way we wouldn't know for sure if she got it. But we still couldn't say a word."

The sober faces in the room remained unsmiling.

"However," Laney went on, "if she tells a few of us, then I think the news could spread naturally from girl to girl. But we couldn't make a big thing of it. Remember, as far as Patch knows, Kate, Ramona, and I have been the only ones who even knew she needed money."

Laney's own optimism waned, seeing the girls struggle with the serious situation. Kate actually looked paler.

As she and Laney walked slowly back to their rooms, Laney felt the weight of the entire scheme resting heavily on her shoulders. "Kate," she said, "would you consider coming with me to talk with Mrs. Church tomorrow? I'd really like to have somebody with me."

"I don't think so, Laney," Kate replied. "You're the ideal person for the job. You're polite, no matter what. I'd probably end up yelling at her, and then the whole thing would fall through."

After the meeting with the girls, Kate had lunch off, and so was free for the afternoon. Gathering up all the money, now carefully sorted and bundled, she taxied to a bank in Fallsburg, where she exchanged it all for paper bills.

―⚬⚬⚬―

The next morning, when Laney arrived in the dining room to work breakfast, she told Ronnie and Patch that she had wakened with a sick headache. Patch's brown eyes grew large with sympathy, as she urged Laney to leave. Ronnie agreed, giving Laney permission with a stony-faced look that defied interpretation.

Then, as Patch prepared to work the busy breakfast alone, Ronnie surprised the girls by reducing her station by two four-seater tables.

Laney thanked them both. Then she walked out quietly. With her head bent and arms wrapped around her middle, she wondered if her lie about feeling sick might possibly come true.

―⚬⚬⚬―

Laney had seen Mrs. Church occasionally over the summer. But she had never spoken with her more than a passing hello. The heavyset and sullen-faced woman was smoking a cigarette as she opened the door of her and Patch's apartment. Glancing dully at Laney in her uniform, she registered mild surprise.

As she led Laney into the small, crowded living room, Laney spied a couch and wondered if it was Patch's bed. From behind walls, laundry machines kept up a dull rumbling.

Laney started out by telling Mrs. Church that the girls had learned about Patch's problem: Patch was registered to start nurse's training the following week, and hadn't been able to save enough money.

The heavy face showed surprise. "She's registered? No, she ain't. Far as I know, she ain't even talked to a hospital."

"Yes, she has," Laney answered. "Patch applied to the hospital in Fallsburg. She just went for her interview, and was accepted. She's to start there next Thursday."

The woman's jaw dropped. "Can't be! Why you tellin' me all this craziness? She ain't smart enough to take nursin'. She ain't fit for nothin' but helpin' with the laundry."

Laney felt heat rising to her face. "That isn't true, Mrs. Church. Patch is one of the best waitresses in the dining room. She's so good, she makes it look easy! I had to struggle to learn! She even helps other girls around her who need help."

The woman responded by pinching her heavy lips shut.

"And she's well-liked," Laney went on. "Everyone likes her. You should be proud of her, Mrs. Church. You have a very nice daughter, and very capable."

Despite the woman's continued silence, Laney forged on. "We like her enough that the girls want to help her get into nurse's training. I have a hundred dollars here." She paused to draw the envelope from her apron pocket. "Actually, it's a hundred and twelve. The girls donated about two dollars each to raise it. Some of them saved the money by ironing their own uniforms."

"So that's why I ain't hardly had no uniforms lately! By rights that money oughta be mine."

"Why? You didn't earn it."

"Well, I'm used to gettin' it!"

Dumbfounded, Laney drew herself up straighter. "Most of this money is from the waitresses," she said. "But a good chunk of it came from Danny. Danny Joyce. He approves of our plan. He even donated money toward it. And Ronnie gave us some money, too."

"You mean, Danny Joyce in the dining room? And that Ronnie?"

"Yes. The management here know about the plan. And they like it."

Mrs. Church's eyes widened at the news.

"Patch has a lot of pride," Laney continued. "We know she won't accept the money from us girls. That's why we're asking you to give it to her. You need to tell her it's from you. She would accept it with thanks, from you."

The woman's brow smoothed somewhat as her face grew calmer. "We're all proud, all us Churches," she said. "All of us works. My man, he's in the coal mines. And my one son."

"I guess that's where Patch learned to be a good worker. From you. Think what a good nurse she'll make."

The woman looked disbelieving again.

Laney suddenly feared that she was failing. "Please, Mrs. Church. I know you love your daughter. Please let her go! Please give her the money! You could tell her you've decided she deserves some help. She'd be so happy."

The woman took a slow breath that lifted the top half of her body. Then she let it out, exuding cigarette smell. Slowly, tentatively, she reached out her hand.

Laney placed the envelope in it. "Don't forget," she said, "you mustn't tell her that I came to see you. And you must tell her that this is a gift from you. Patch won't accept it any other way."

Slowly nodding, the woman opened the envelope to peer in at the money.

Laney waited a moment longer. Then, in the woman's continued silence, she thanked her kindly and left.

———

Rain fell steadily that night, but by dawn it had nearly stopped. When Laney stepped out of the dorm, the alley smelled like fresh-washed asphalt with a delicate trace of honeysuckle. She had come outside half an hour earlier than usual. After hurrying through the light rain to the cafeteria, she stepped under the roof overhang. Then, turning to face the dorm, she watched and waited for Patch to emerge.

In a short while, Patch stepped off the dorm porch. Seeing Laney, she started toward her. Walking with her head down, she was just a few yards from Laney before she lifted her face. It looked as if she had been crying.

Then came the grin that stretched wide and made Patch's plain face beautiful. "Guess what, Laney. You'll never guess what happened."

"What? Tell me!"

"I'm gonna report to the hospital next week! I act'ully have enough money!"

"What...? Well, how...," Laney stammered. *No tears!*

"Mom gave it to me! I can hardly b'lieve it! She gave me a hundred and fifteen bucks! I'm gonna have more than five hundred after Labor Day. Maybe I can even get a new outfit or two. Though I prob'ly won't need 'em...."

"Patch, I'm so happy for you!"

Laney grabbed both of her arms and shook them. Then they locked arms and jumped up and down together, laughing and tearful.

"Somethin' else," Patch muttered, facing down again. "My Mom just told me she was proud of me. That may not sound like much to you...."

"No, that's wonderful, Patch! I know how wonderful that is!"

"What's happening?" Kate yelled from the dorm porch. "What are you two crazies doing?"

"Come on over! Patch has some news!" Laney called back.

As Kate and Ramona came running through the drizzle, three more girls appeared behind them on the dorm porch.

"Hey!" one girl yelled. "What's everyone hollering about?"

"Come over and find out," Laney called.

Kate and Ramona reached the cafeteria, followed by the three others. Patch quietly explained to the three girls her need for money, and then told them all about her mother's gift. The air around them became so electrified with joy, no resistance from Patch could prevent the happy shouting. More girls were on their way, running from the dorm.

"Let's go in and have some coffee," Laney said. "I'm so cold and wet, I've got goosebumps!"

"Hey, they've got those little sausages!" said Patch, wiping her cheeks. "How'd they know we was celebratin'?"

"We *were* celebrating, Patch," Laney corrected her.

"We *were* celebratin'," Patch repeated. "And we still are!"

"Guess what?" Laney shouted to her as they all crowded in. "Remember the guy I was afraid to serve dinner to? Mom just told me he was a boy I dated, years ago."

"I told you he wasn't bad lookin'!" Patch replied. "You wouldn't listen!"

"I know," Laney answered. "I was a scared rabbit."

"This is the start of the Labor Day weekend," someone remembered. "We're going to run our legs off today, girls."

"One of the men said the parking lot is packed!"
"I don't care, I'm so happy for Patch—"
"Me too! This is going to be a wonderful day!"
"Hurray! We're soon going home!"
"Somebody hand me a plate," said Patch.

———✖———

Esther Escott is a former art teacher, and continues to work in pastels and other media. The pencil illustrations in this book are her own.

Escott and her husband have lead a hiking group through the Sierra foothills and mountains, which, combined with her visits to Mexico, have provided her with ample inspiration for her pastel paintings.

Esther and her husband have two sons and four grandchildren. She has a bachelor's degree in art education from UPI in Pennsylvania.

www.ingramcontent.com/pod-product-compliance
Lightning Source LLC
Chambersburg PA
CBHW070849120626
46556CB00002B/933